Screamfang was planning a three-hundred-thousand-dollar heist less than twenty feet away from me. I reached into my pocket and pulled out my crisis monitor, which Keystone had given me a week earlier. Unfortunately, I hadn't bothered to figure out how to use it to report crises yet.

"I need you to do me a favor," Screamfang told the clerk. "Go dial 911. Tell them Screamfang—that's 'scream' as in 'Aaaaaah!' and 'fang' as in 'chomp'—is stealing a truck full of air conditioners. Think you can do that for me?"

"Y-y-yes, sir," the clerk stammered.

"Great. While you're doing that, I'm going to bust up the joint a little bit. Cause a ruckus, you know? Cool?"

The clerk nervously scampered away. Screamfang walked to the end of the aisle, which was where all the lighting fixtures and ceiling fans were on display. He took a deep breath. It didn't occur to me what he had planned until it was too late.

READ THEM ALL!

#1: SECRET IDENTITY CRISIS
#2: FREEZER BURNED
#3: RED ALERT
#4: THE COMIC CON

THE COMIC CON

by

JAKE BELL

cover and comic art by
CHRIS GIARRUSSO

SCHOLASTIC INC.

New York Toronto London Auc

Sydney Mexico City New Delhi H

For Theresa, Teacher Dave, Mr. Dell'Ergo,
Mr. Wheeler, Miss Tarkoff, and all the other
teachers who helped me get here.

(Especially the ones who put up with kids reading my books
in class when they should be paying attention . . .)

No part of this publication may be reproduced, stored in a retrieval system, or transmitted in any form or by any means, electronic, mechanical, photocopying, recording, or otherwise, without written permission of the publisher. For information regarding permission, write to Scholastic Inc., Attention: Permissions Department, 557 Broadway, New York, NY 10012.

ISBN 978-0-545-15672-1

Text copyright © 2011 by Jake Bell
Illustrations copyright © 2011 by Scholastic Inc.
All rights reserved. Published by Scholastic Inc.
SCHOLASTIC, APPLE PAPERBACKS, THE AMAZING
ADVENTURES OF NATE BANKS, and associated logos are
trademarks and/or registered trademarks of Scholastic Inc.

12 11 10 9 8 7 6 5 4 3 2 1   11 12 13 14 15 16/0

Printed in the U.S.A.   40
First printing, February 2011

Contents

1. Donut Stop Believin'............................1

2. Good Spinal Hygiene, Kids! 9

3. That's "Scream" as in "Aaaaaah!".............15

4. Supergrammar...................................23

5. To the Janitor's Closet!.......................32

6. 28.6 Seconds...................................38

7. More Than a Million...for a Comic Book?......44

8. This Place Is a Zoo............................51

9. Rhinos Don't Bite..............................58

10. They Make Great Pets..........................65

11. Big Bucks for Mint Condition...................73

12. Jailbreak......................................79

13. Mayhem...86

14. We'll Open the Bidding at Two Million........93

15. Conventional Wisdom...........................100

16. That's How I Roll.............................106

17. Facts and (Action) Figures...................115

18. The Final Frontier............................123

19. Not Please—*Police*...........................129

20. Never Make a Deal with a Supervillain.......136

21. You Mess with the Con........................145

22. Not Worth a Nickel...........................152

Donut Stop Believin'

It was a typical Thursday afternoon—or at least what had become typical for me—and I was training in the damp cave that served as Doctor Nocturne's secret headquarters. Out of the corner of my eye, I spotted a fuzzy yellow blur headed in my direction. I had to bend my knees to maintain my balance while I leaned backward, allowing the tennis ball to sail harmlessly past my chin. Quickly, I straightened up and focused on the four TV monitors in front of me, their images cycling every few seconds.

Three sprinters reached the finish line at the same time, a man hailed a taxi, a flag fluttered in the breeze, and a scared cartoon pig stared out his window at an angry wolf on his doorstep. One at a time, the images changed. The image of the flag became one of a lizard darting its long tongue out to nab a dragonfly, and a second later, the image of the little pig in the house made of sticks switched to an image of three kids playing soccer.

Another tennis ball headed toward my legs. I leapt off the narrow stone pillar where I stood, relying on my legs to find their own way back onto the small, flattened surface. By now, I hardly ever fell, even when I wasn't looking. And I rarely looked, since I didn't dare take my eyes off the monitors.

My left shoe hit a patch of moss that was growing on the flattened stalagmite, but my right leg instinctively adjusted itself to support my weight until I had a more solid footing.

For two months, I had been training every Monday and Thursday after school. I'd gone from struggling just to stand upright on one of the slippery, slimy stalagmites to jumping easily from one stalagmite to another. Even so, every training session seemed more difficult than the last.

After I spent almost four minutes dodging, leaping, and ducking while keeping my eyes on the hundreds of pictures and video clips on the monitors, my legs couldn't take any more. I saw the tennis ball heading toward my chest, but when I rolled my shoulder away from it, the heel of my shoe slipped off the stalagmite, and the rest of my body followed.

Lying on my back, I stared up into the impatient face of

the man I used to know as Doctor Nocturne. A few weeks earlier, he had officially passed on the name and the duties as Kurtzburg's resident superhero to his daughter. He now went by the name Keystone. The Phantom Ranger had suggested it because the former Doc Noc was an essential part of the superhero community, providing training, equipment, and support to anyone who needed it.

Also, Keystone sounded better than his real name, which was Orpheus.

"How many people did you see wearing blue shirts?" Keystone asked with his gruff Southern accent. "What was the license plate number on the white pickup truck? Where did the man drinking the coffee buy it?"

"Blue? I think seven. Maybe eight," I answered. "The license plate on the white one started with a four. Four NW . . . J, maybe? Then I think five-seven-six. And if you're talking about the guy who was hailing the taxi, his coffee cup said 'Donut Stop Believin'.'"

Keystone set his jaw and frowned slightly, offering a hand to help me up. "Close enough, I guess."

I smiled, knowing that "Close enough, I guess" translated to "Wow, great job! I'm very proud of you!" in Keystone-ese.

With a tug, Keystone pulled me to my feet. He might have been retired from day-to-day crime fighting, but you'd never guess it from looking at him. Apart from a few gray hairs and the cane he leaned on, Keystone would have fit in alongside any superhero you could name. With his broad chest, powerful arms, and stern, chiseled facial features, Keystone looked about half his age.

The same couldn't be said for Hubert.

Once upon a time, before my dad was born, Hubert had been a superhero named the Dart. He'd long since hung up his uniform and settled down in a condo in Florida. But then, two months ago, a little incident with the supervillain Red Malice had pulled him out of retirement for one last showdown.

When I first met Hubert, we were in a hospital, and I mistakenly assumed he was a patient. His withered old body leaned desperately on a walker, and tubes from an oxygen tank ran up into his nose. They didn't seem to do much good, though, since he couldn't make it through two sentences without taking a break for a deep, rattling gasp.

That made it all the more surprising when he had run from Maryland to California in less than ten minutes. He could have done it faster, too, if he hadn't stopped to change clothes in Florida.

The Dart's superspeed came from the Ring of Mercury, an ancient artifact that he'd passed along to Fiona, one of my best friends, during the showdown with

Red Malice. Now Keystone was training her, too. She was currently blazing along around at six hundred miles an hour on a treadmill—or something that resembled a treadmill but had jet engines attached. The two turbines spun the reinforced belt at nearly supersonic speeds. Even though sound dampeners were built into the engines, the entire cave echoed with the whine of Fiona's superspeed training device.

"Balance!" Hubert shouted over the racket. "The most important thing to a speedster is balance." He wheezed and coughed from the effort it took to shout over the roar of the turbines. "Don't worry about going faster— hhhheeeehhhh—worry about going straighter."

Fiona had no trouble with speed. In fact, she struggled to go slowly enough to stay on her feet. She needed to learn to control herself. When she ran, it looked as though her upper body was trying to stay attached to legs that were barreling forward at an insane speed.

When I'd met Hubert, my hand had brushed against the Ring of Mercury for a split second. I had instantly had a nearly uncontrollable urge to run anywhere, in any direction. Just touching the ring for a second had left me completely exhausted, so I couldn't imagine what wearing it on my finger would be like.

Keystone pulled the large switch that supplied power

to the treadmill, and the cave filled with a long whine as the turbines spun to a stop. Fiona stumbled as the path beneath her slowed. She slipped off the end of the belt and collapsed on the ground, desperately clawing the ring from her finger and dropping it on the stone floor.

"Balance," Hubert reminded her. "If you're leaning half an inch to either side, you're going to be two miles off course after a minute's run."

With a shaking hand, he offered her a box of raisins from his fanny pack. She snatched it without a word, shredded the top, and dumped them all into her mouth at once.

"Remember what I told you," he said. "Eat lots of potassium—hhhheeeehhhh—raisins, lima beans, potatoes, and squash. Superspeed drains it right out of you."

As Fiona chewed, her eyes widened, almost like she was waking up from a nap. "Thanks," she whispered hoarsely.

"What's next?" I asked Keystone as he handed Fiona a bottle of water, which she emptied in seconds.

"Next, you guys head home," he said. "It's almost five o'clock in Kanigher Falls."

Fiona and I made eye contact long enough to share a relieved sigh.

"You're both coming along, but you have a long way

to go," Keystone grumbled. That was one of the highest compliments I'd ever heard him give us. "Now pack up and head upstairs."

I had nothing to pack, but Fiona carefully strung the Ring of Mercury onto a chain she wore around her neck, trying to touch the dark blue metal ring as little as possible.

The entrance to Keystone's secret cavern is hidden along the craggy coast of Gerber Bay. To get in directly from the outside, you need to maneuver a narrow road along the cliffs that skirt the bay, wind down a tight tunnel, and cross a wide chasm. A car is too wide to fit through the tunnel, and a person could never leap across the chasm, so a motorcycle is the only option.

But since there were four of us, we had to use the other entrance, a long pneumatic elevator that runs from the rear of the cave up into the kitchen pantry of Orpheus Duncan's palatial mansion. One at a time, we took the ride, like bullets fired back to the surface world.

Every room in the mansion was dark. Even when you entered a room and the lights came on—triggered by a motion sensor—they were dim and kept the corners hidden in inky blackness. Occasionally, you'd see a framed photograph of a younger Keystone with his daughter before she became Doctor Nocturne, or the baseball bat that hung above the fireplace in the living room, but mostly you saw darkness.

Not that we had much time to see anything, no matter what the lighting was like. Keystone hurried us through the house to the garage, which was about the size of a museum. Fiona and I crawled into the backseat of a gray sedan while Hubert wrestled with his walker, trying to get into the front seat.

Keystone started the car. "When you get home, do your homework, get a good night's rest, and stay out of trouble until next week," he ordered us as he backed out of the garage.

Good Spinal
Hygiene, Kids!

Keystone dropped us off in the Kurtzburg Cemetery, and we helped Hubert up the hill to a white marble crypt with ZUEMBAY engraved on it. Fiona pushed open the door, and together we guided the old man down the steps into the heart of the tomb.

A decapitated corpse was seated on the floor, its decaying neck exposing the vertebrae for us to see clearly. All three of us recoiled in shock.

"Oh, are you guys back already?" asked Captain Zombie's head, which was sitting on top of a marble and brass bar. His body got to its feet and ambled over to take a seat on one of the barstools.

"What happened to you?" Fiona cried.

My friend Teddy stood up from behind the bar with a dirty toothbrush in his hand. "Okay, found it," he told Captain Zombie's head.

"Could you do my neck first?" Captain Zombie requested. Teddy nodded and came around from behind the bar. Then he began scrubbing the top of the exposed spine. "You'll have to excuse me being a bad host," Captain Zombie apologized. "Help yourself to some Chinese food on the table. The kung pao shrimp is the best you'll find anywhere. And there are sodas in the fridge. I'd get them for you, but I'm indisposed right now." His body shrugged.

I thanked him but knew my dad would be making dinner soon. Fiona had no such reservations. She dumped a pile of fried rice onto a plate and began wolfing it down.

"I'd love to join you," Hubert wheezed while patting his stomach, "but anything spicier than cottage cheese—hhhheeeehhhh—and I'll be up all night." He took a long inhale of his oxygen. "My bus should be coming. Can you . . . ?" He pointed back to the stairs.

"Of course." Captain Zombie smiled. "Next stop, sunny Florida."

Since Fiona was eating and Teddy was brushing, I helped Hubert up the stairs to catch his bus and get home.

In addition to being the resident superhero of Haney, Captain Zombie provided a valuable service to other heroes. His Power of the Graveyard wasn't restricted to just one graveyard. In fact, it extended to every cemetery in the world, and his mausoleum was a nexus that managed to exist simultaneously in every one of them. This meant that you could step through the door in Kurtzburg and step out in Kanigher Falls—or Florida, or anywhere else, for that matter—just a second later.

I took a moment to breathe in the salty ocean air while helping Hubert to the bus stop just outside the cemetery. When I returned to the crypt, Fiona had moved on to a second helping of Chinese food, and Teddy now had Captain Zombie's head cradled upside down in his left arm while he vigorously brushed the base of the neck with the toothbrush.

"But he wasn't alone," Captain Zombie was telling Fiona. "I didn't even see who all was there, but the next thing I know, I'm in the street."

"What did I miss?" I asked.

"Captain Zombie ran into some supervillains when he went out to get the Chinese food," Fiona informed me through a mouth stuffed with walnut prawns. "Sawhorse and some other guys."

"And he cut off your head?!" I exclaimed.

"No, no, no," the upside-down head of Captain Zombie said. "There were a bunch of them, actually. One of the big bruisers punched my head off. Maybe it was

Antisocialite or Schoolboy Krush. I think I saw the Puritan there, too."

"Doesn't that seem weird?" I asked. "Why would a bunch of supervillains be hanging out at a Chinese restaurant in the Midwest?"

"Have you tried their kung pao?" Captain Zombie asked. "It's to die for."

Fiona nodded vigorously. "It really is great," she mumbled, her mouth stuffed.

That wasn't quite what I'd meant, but before I could make my point, Teddy interrupted.

"Okay, I think I'm done," he announced as he blew gently on the base of Captain Zombie's skull and examined it closely.

"Thanks, Teddy," Captain Zombie said. His body turned on its stool and held out its arms. "Hand me over."

Captain Zombie grabbed his head in his hands and placed it back on his neck. Carefully, he squared everything up just right, then pushed down fast and hard with a sickening crunch. Fiona gagged.

"Sorry about that," Captain Zombie said as he stretched his neck and rolled his head around to test it. "Ah, that's much better. Thank you again, Teddy."

"No prob," my friend answered.

"What were you doing?" I asked Teddy.

"When my head got knocked off, it fell in the street," Captain Zombie explained. "I popped it back on, but I don't know if there was a pebble in there or what. You know what it feels like when you get a stone in your shoe? Well, imagine that in your neck."

I winced.

"Fortunately, Teddy was here," Captain Zombie continued, taking the toothbrush from Teddy. "You have no idea how difficult it is to clean your own neck. You know why?"

"Because your eyes are in your own head?" Fiona guessed without looking up from her plate.

"Exactly." He gestured toward us with the toothbrush before dropping it into a drawer. "Good spinal hygiene, kids. You take it for granted until you lose it."

Captain Zombie wrapped up his story. He'd managed to call on the Power of the Graveyard to summon the zombified remains of a squad of long-dead police officers for help in catching the bad guys. He'd stopped Colosso himself, and a few others were in jail, but he suspected that at least a few had gotten away. "I'll go check in with the Haney police for all the details after you guys head home," he said.

"Which we should probably do," I suggested. "My dad'll be home in about twenty minutes, and if I'm not there doing my homework, he's going to want to know why."

Fiona paused in mid-chew and nodded reluctantly. She grabbed three egg rolls and dropped them into her jacket pocket.

"It was good seeing you all again," Captain Zombie said, the gracious host as always. "Teddy, I'm sorry we didn't get to play gin rummy because of the whole neck thing."

"That's okay," Teddy assured him. "Unless I get some superpowers in the next couple of days, we'll have plenty of time to play next week."

That's "Scream" as in "Aaaaaah!"

After dinner, my dad needed to run to the hardware store. He promised me that if I went with him and helped load the plywood he was buying into his car, he wouldn't make me do flash cards for a week. I don't know how many boxes of flash cards my dad's purchased in my lifetime, but I know he bought my first set—which had letters and pictures of words that started with each letter—before I was born.

I agreed to go with him, but not to get out of doing flash cards. Since Keystone had started testing how quickly I could recognize and remember images, flash cards were a breeze. In fact, I wondered whether all those years of Dad making me do flash cards had helped with my training in the cave.

We started with a few sheets of plywood, but whenever

I go shopping with my dad, I can count on him to buy about ten extra things.

"I don't know how many screws we have," he said. "We should probably pick some up just to be sure."

After he spent five minutes picking out the right box of screws, he remembered that the battery on the drill wasn't holding a charge anymore. Then he debated just buying a new drill, as long as he was looking at drill batteries. This went on and on until we stepped outside into the garden area. I sat in a cedar lawn chair while Dad read the ingredients on the sides of forty-pound bags of soil.

"I don't get it," Dad complained. "I don't see any difference in the contents, but this one is almost twice as expensive."

I got up and wandered for a little while, knowing that Dad wouldn't come to a decision on the soil anytime soon.

Back just inside the doorway of the store, a man was looking at an air conditioner.

"This is the top of the line, sir," a clerk told him. "It's Swedish."

"Ten thousand dollars, huh?" the man asked. "And that's the most expensive thing you have in the store?"

"Yes, sir."

"Ten thousand?"

"I'm sorry, sir, but we can't go any lower. This is a new product. We got them in today. We haven't even had time to unload the truck out back."

The man seemed to perk up. "A truck full of ten-thousand-dollar air conditioners? How many air conditioners fit in one truck?"

"I'd have to check that," the clerk answered suspiciously. "Probably about thirty or so."

"Thirty ten-thousand-dollar air conditioners," the man said. "I guess that's about three hundred thousand dollars, huh?"

"Yes, sir."

"Okay, I think that'll do."

"I'm sorry, sir? Did you want to buy all thirty?"

"No," the man laughed. "I want to *steal* all thirty. Now, the smart thing would have been for me to sneak out back and take the truck when nobody's looking, but for this particular job, I can't do that."

The man took off his jacket and hat, and my mouth fell open even before he smiled, revealing two full rows of teeth sharpened to points.

Screamfang was planning a three-hundred-thousand-dollar heist less than twenty feet away from me. I reached into my pocket and pulled out my crisis monitor, which

Keystone had given me a week earlier. Ultraviolet had one just like it. The thin, flat video screen was about the size of my hand. It monitored all police and emergency channels, satellite communications, and television broadcasts and alerted us to any dangers that might need Ultraviolet's attention.

Unfortunately, I hadn't bothered to figure out how to use it to *report* crises.

"I need you to do me a favor," Screamfang told the clerk. "Go dial 911. Tell them Screamfang—that's 'scream' as in 'Aaaaaah!' and 'fang' as in 'chomp'—is stealing a truck full of air conditioners. Think you can do that for me?"

"Y-y-yes, sir," the clerk stammered.

"Great. While you're doing that, I'm going to bust up the joint a little bit. Cause a ruckus, you know? Cool?"

The clerk nervously scampered away. Screamfang walked to the end of the aisle, which was where all the lighting fixtures and ceiling fans were on display. He took a deep breath. It didn't occur to me what he had planned until it was too late.

A deafening shriek echoed off the concrete walls of the store, doubling back on itself. Every lightbulb and piece of glass in the lighting display shattered simultaneously in a miniature fireworks display.

I pressed my fingers into my ears a second after the scream began, but the damage had already been done. My ears rang with a constant high-pitched whine, which would stay with me most of the night.

Screamfang stopped screaming and casually stepped out the door into the garden center. I figured he was heading toward the loading docks, where the trucks parked.

The crisis monitor in my pocket vibrated furiously. I'd had it for a week and it had never done this before. This warning was different from the others I'd seen, too. **SUPERPOWER ACTIVITY DETECTED**, it read in bold white letters. A red dot flashed on a map of Kanigher Falls. I didn't have to zoom in to recognize that it was indicating the exact spot where I was standing.

I hurried back to find my dad, who was looking for me.

"What was that?" he asked.

"Supervillain named Screamfang," I told him.

"What?" he yelled, rubbing his ears with his fingers as if trying to dig something out of them.

Before I could answer, a streak of white and purple descended from the sky and landed in the middle of the perennial flowers in the garden center. Ultraviolet, the superhero defender of Kanigher Falls, had arrived. She was superstrong, she could fly, and she could withstand any pain. For months I had been both Ultraviolet's advisor on all things superhero-related and a student in her sixth-grade history class. Screamfang had made a terrible mistake. You did not mess with Ultraviolet—or Ms. Matthews, for that matter.

"So you're Ultraviolet?" Screamfang hooted. "This should be easy."

He took a deep breath.

"Ultraviolet!" I shouted. "Your ears!"

Unfortunately, my advice seemed to distract her more than help her. Before she could register what I had said, Screamfang screamed again. Even though I had my fingers in my ears, it was deafening. Ultraviolet fell to one knee, and Screamfang rushed toward her, swinging a forty-pound bag of manure at her head.

It doesn't matter how strong or invulnerable you are—when someone hits you with forty pounds of manure while you're off balance on one knee with your hands in your ears, you *will* fall down. Ultraviolet was laid out on the cement, but quickly jumped back up.

Screamfang shrieked again, and it soon became apparent that Ultraviolet could plug her ears or fight him, but not both.

He swung again, and this time she dodged the bag of manure. Screamfang laughed like a kid playing a game.

Another swing of the bag followed. Finally, Ultraviolet threw up her left elbow and caught the plastic bag, tearing it open and sending cow manure in a fanlike pattern across the ground.

I looked at the small clumps that rolled over near my feet and was inspired. I took my fingers out of my ears and crouched to shove in two soft, squishy lumps of fertilizer. My dinner welled up in my throat, but I managed to keep it down.

I popped back up and hurried toward the flowers and other plants. My father might have yelled for me to stop, but I didn't hear him if he did.

Through the lumps of manure, I could barely hear another scream. My ears were totally sealed off. A quick scan of the display revealed exactly what I needed.

Screamfang laughed some more as he screamed in Ultraviolet's face again.

I snuck up behind him and picked up a ceramic bowl full of baby cacti. With everything I had, I launched it into the back of Screamfang's head.

He continued to scream, but it sounded different now. Instead of shrieking aggressively, he yowled in pain. Ultraviolet was able to uncork a right cross that dropped him to the cement like a marionette whose strings someone had cut.

Police arrived on the scene with their lights flashing, and Ultraviolet mouthed the words "thank you" to me before she flew off.

I headed home with my dad, a long night of scrubbing and cotton swabs ahead.

Supergrammar

"Nate Banks, please see me after class," my English teacher, Mr. Dawson, announced as we filed out of the room. I gave Teddy a wave and said I'd see him at lunch, then approached the teacher's desk warily. I'd been steadily improving my grades since the start of the school year and couldn't think of any assignments I hadn't turned in, so I wasn't sure what he wanted.

Mr. Dawson waited until the other students were gone, then closed the door to the classroom.

"Nate, I have a question for you," he said quietly. "You are obviously well versed in the world of superheroes."

I already sensed where this conversation was going, so I cut him off. "Mr. Dawson, I know there have been rumors about Ultraviolet and I—"

"Ultraviolet and me," he corrected me. "In this case, you are the object of the sentence, not the subject. It's simple. Just take out the other person and say it again. You wouldn't say, 'There have been rumors about I,' would you?"

"Uh, I guess not," I replied. "My point was I really don't know Ultraviolet that well. I can't get you an autograph."

"Oh, no, I don't want an autograph, Nate." He tented his fingers and leaned forward nervously. "I have to ask you—can we keep this conversation in the strictest confidence?"

I didn't answer, because I wasn't sure what he meant.

"Can we keep it a secret?" he asked. "Just between you and me?"

"Oh, yeah. Sure. I guess."

"Wonderful," he sighed with relief. "Nate, I need to know about superheroes."

This made me a little nervous. A few months earlier, our science teacher, Dr. Content, had tried to draw upon my superhero knowledge, and he wound up destroying the school and trying to kill me in the process.

"How . . . how does a superhero know when he has superpowers?" Mr. Dawson whispered.

The question caught me by surprise. I'd never really thought about it before. "I don't know," I admitted. "I would think it's pretty obvious when you start flying around or lifting cars—"

He raised a hand to cut me off. "What about situations where the powers might be less apparent? For example, we accept that if someone can run two hundred miles per hour, then that person has superspeed, because it is beyond the capability of even the fastest athletes. Isn't it possible that a person might have an unquantifiable power that is superhuman without anyone else noticing?"

I was confused. "I'm not sure what you mean," I said.

"'Unquantifiable' means you can't measure it," he explained.

My stomach was rumbling, so I cut to the chase. "What superpowers do you think you—"

My voice was drowned out by a fit of faked coughing, which was followed by Mr. Dawson desperately peering around the empty room to make sure no one had heard me. "Please, keep your voice down," he said.

"Sorry," I whispered.

"I think I have supergrammar."

Mr. Dawson sat back in his chair proudly. I didn't know how to respond. Was he serious?

"Well, you're right," I said hesitantly. "There's no way to really measure—"

"Ah!" he snapped. "That's a split infinitive. You should have said, 'There's no accurate way to measure.' See what

I mean, Nate? I see grammatical errors everywhere. In today's newspaper, there was an article that incorrectly used 'lay' instead of 'lie,' and another that used the term 'for all intensive purposes.'"

I shrugged. I wasn't sure what intensive purposes were, but I figured it was just one of those weird expressions.

"The proper term is 'for all *intents and* purposes,'" Mr. Dawson continued. "And I'm guessing you've noticed my propensity to correct you and your classmates?"

I nodded in agreement, assuming that "propensity" meant he did it a lot.

"Nate, I understand this might sound a bit crazy. Everybody and their mother-in-laws probably wish they had superpowers, right?"

"I suppose so—"

"Trick question!" he said, zinging me. "The plural of 'mother-in-law' is '*mothers*-in-law'! It's like 'attorneys general' or—"

"Mr. Dawson," I interrupted him. "Let's just assume you do have supergrammar. Did you have a question for me?"

He smirked at me as though it was obvious. "Whom do I talk to about becoming a superhero?"

o o o

Moments later, I was standing in line in the cafeteria with Teddy, explaining my weird conversation with Mr. Dawson.

"I still don't understand," Teddy said. "Why can't they just be mother-in-laws?"

"I don't know," I said. "I guess it just sounds smarter. My point was that he wants to be a superhero who tells people they're talking wrong."

"Smarter, huh?" Teddy said with a thoughtful look.

The lunch line inched forward, and Teddy leaned in to get his food. "I'll have the chickens finger," he declared loudly with a British accent. "And for my vegetable, can I have both the taters tot and the carrots stick?"

He shot me a knowing glance and smiled. Because he was looking at me, Teddy didn't see the lunch lady shake her head as she filled his tray.

"I think it's working," he announced.

"I think you're doing it wrong," I disagreed.

Teddy got his tray and we started toward the table where Fiona was sitting with Mark and Robby. She had already started eating from the three trays in front of her. "Hey, guys, wait up," Dave Bargman called as he ran up behind us. "You guys are going to Kanigher Kon, right?"

The city's annual comic-book convention was only

a week away. Once a year, comic-book collectors, publishers, writers, artists, and store owners filled the convention hall at the Kanigher Falls Collins Inn. Well, maybe not "filled," but there were a few hundred of us. It might not have been as big as the Darwyn City Con or Weisinger World, but it was the only thing we had.

The rest of the room was filled with fans of other science fiction and fantasy stuff, with everything divided into its own area. There were rows of tables staffed by people selling old comics, toys, shirts, posters, models, DVDs, and more. A few comic publishers even brought in some artists or writers to sign autographs. This would be my third year attending, and I'd been setting aside Christmas and birthday money for months in preparation.

Some celebrities usually showed up and sat behind a table in the back corner with their arms crossed, ignoring everyone until someone agreed to pay twenty bucks for an autographed picture.

The fans of Japanese cartoons and comics, anime and manga, had a section to themselves, and so did the cosplayers—people who made costumes to dress up like their favorite superheroes, villains, or characters. But everyone wound up wandering around and mixing together.

"Of course we're going," Teddy said as he sat down at the table. "We bought our convention tickets—er, I mean our conventions ticket—two months ago."

"Conventions ticket?" Dave repeated, looking confused.

"Just let it go," I advised him.

"Are you guys going to LARP?" he asked excitedly.

Teddy, Fiona, and I exchanged ignorant glances, each wondering who would ask the inevitable question.

Fiona shrugged. "What's a larp?" she asked gamely.

"Live-Action Role-Playing," Dave replied as if she'd asked for a recipe for peanut butter and jelly sandwiches. "You guys have never heard of LARPing? It's taking role-playing games to the next level. Instead of sitting at a table, rolling dice, you put on costumes and act out the game."

"And roll dice?" Teddy asked.

"Well, yeah."

"That's stupid. You get into a fight and you settle it by rolling dice? That would never work in real life," Teddy complained. "I thought this was a comic-book convention. Why are they having role-playing games?"

"It's a comic-book and science fiction convention," I corrected him. "That means a little of everything."

"You guys with your comics and you with your . . . whatever," Mark said, mocking us.

"LARP," Dave reminded us.

"Yeah, lerp," Mark continued. "What a bunch of weirdos."

Robby piped up. "What are you talking about? You said you were going to the con, too."

"Yeah, but I'm going for the *Galactic Journey* stuff," Mark argued. "Sven Ryan is going to be there signing his biography."

"Is he the one who blew up the *Doomstar*?" I asked, trying to keep a straight face.

"The *Doomstar* was in *Cosmic Combat*," Mark snapped. "It's a totally different thing." Fans of *Cosmic Combat* hated *Galactic Journey,* and fans of *Galactic Journey* hated *Cosmic Combat.*

Of course, I had already known that. But it never stopped being funny how upset either side would get if you pretended not to know the difference.

"Are you going to wear your *Galactic Journey* uniform?" Teddy asked Mark.

"Sure, but I can't decide if I should wear the blue shirt or the red shirt."

"Good thing you have a week to think it over," Fiona said before covering her mouth and fake coughing, "Weirdo!"

We all laughed while Mark scowled.

I opened my lunch bag to see what my dad had packed me, but before I could take the first bite of my sandwich, I was interrupted by a vibration in my pocket. A constant stream of events flashed across the crisis monitor's video screen, but if something of immediate importance happened, I was alerted with a silent vibration.

I reached into my pocket but couldn't take the monitor out in front of Dave and the others. Teddy and Fiona saw my concerned look and my hand in my pocket and made the connection.

"Again?" Fiona asked.

"What again?" Dave wondered.

"Um, yeah," I said nervously.

"What's wrong?" Robby asked with concern.

"Nate, um . . ." Teddy searched for an excuse. "Nate has diarrhea," he announced loudly.

I glared at Teddy in silence. "Nate has to go to the bathroom" probably would have done the job, but Teddy wasn't known for his subtlety. Embarrassed, I didn't have time to come up with a new excuse.

No doubt Ultraviolet was already on the case.

"I have to go," I said, and started for her hidden lair, which was conveniently located right underneath the school.

To the Janitor's Closet!

I raced across the courtyard to the main building and down the social studies wing. The monitor screen showed a map of downtown with a flashing red dot over a silhouette of a house near city hall. It was registering as another supervillain attack, but I figured that had to be a mistake. In the entire history of Kanigher Falls prior to that week, there had been two supervillain attacks. What were the chances of two within two days?

After a quick, precautionary glance around to make sure no one was looking, I slipped into the janitor's closet. I stepped into what appeared to be a basin for the janitor to empty his mop bucket and gave the hot water faucet a tap with my foot. In an instant, I plummeted five stories down an elevator shaft into Ultraviolet's secret base of operations.

One of the dozens of computer monitors flashed the

same red dot as my handheld monitor but provided a continually updated list of alerts on the left side of the screen. I tried to keep up with the list as I slipped on a microphone headset. According to the screen I was focusing on, DeFalco Mansion, the mayor's home, had been broken into by . . . tiny robots?

"The last report from Mayor Van Slyke's personal security system mentioned tiny robots," I told Ultraviolet through the headset. "That was four minutes ago, and there hasn't been an update since."

"Any ideas what that might mean?" she replied, already at the the mayor's home. "What supervillain uses tiny robots?"

"I'm trying to think of somebody," I said. Toysaurus Rex used remote control cars and planes, so it was possible he was using remote control robots.

"I'm going inside," Ultraviolet said. "Anything I should know?"

"None of the security cameras inside the mansion are showing me anything," I replied.

I thought hard about supervillains who used robots. Roboa Constrictor had a robotic snake, but it was thirty feet long.

"I see two of the security guards," Ultraviolet reported. "They look like they're covered in cotton candy or—"

"Spiderwebs?" I snapped back. "Terrorantula!"

But before I could give her any further warning, I saw her stagger into view on one of the DeFalco Mansion security cameras. She was clutching at thin, sticky strands of webbing that obscured her trademark purple goggles and clogged her nose and mouth.

Terrorantula stepped into the picture as well. With a wave of his hand, a swarm of robotic spiders spilled out the doorway behind him and covered Ultraviolet. Each one shot out a strand of webbing to anchor itself to a wall, the floor, a banister, or the stairs. Ultraviolet's super-strength would easily outmatch any of the spiderbots, but with so many pulling her in every direction at once, it looked like she was struggling to stay on her feet.

After a few seconds of self-congratulatory observation, Terrorantula mockingly buffed the spider emblem on his shoulder, flashed a thumbs-up at the security camera, and held up a piece of paper that he then folded and tucked into his belt.

"You need to get out of there!" I shouted into the earpiece microphone. "The longer you stay there, the stronger those spiderbots' grip is going to get. They're anchoring themselves. Terrorantula's webbing is thin, but it's strong."

Ultraviolet dropped to one knee while the laughing

supervillain held up a device and pressed a button. Then he fled out the front door.

I glanced at one of the screens showing the external view of the mayor's mansion. It looked like the police had been setting up for a standoff, but they didn't seem to have anticipated Terrorantula's method of escape. A two-story-tall robotic spider crushed eight police cars at once on its way to the front door to pick up its master. When someone on the police force finally got over the initial shock of the scene and gave the order to fire, bullets ricocheted harmlessly off the robot's armor. Terrorantula laughed.

"He's boarding a large spider-shaped vehicle," I told Ultraviolet as I watched her crouch on the mayor's marble floor. I knew that the longer the webbing stayed attached to her, the harder it would be for her to break free. I wished I could do something other than watch her slowly collapse on the screen.

Finally, she managed to jerk her right arm across her body. While the strands of webbing didn't break, the banister to the stairs did. With that arm free at last, she gripped the now-solid gray mask across her face and peeled it off, taking several deep breaths.

She stepped forward, dragging a table behind her that was anchored by the hundreds of hardened strands of webbing. A chunk of the plaster wall to her left crumbled in her wake as well. Free to move both arms, she raised her hands to her goggles and started to remove them.

"Turn around," I warned her. "I can see your face on the security feed."

She waved to acknowledge she'd heard me, then turned away, cleaning off the lenses. A few of the spiderbots shot out more webs in an attempt to resecure Ultraviolet, but the majority seemed to recognize the futility of the attempt, loosened their grips, and scurried away, disappearing into cracks in the walls of the mansion.

Outside the mansion, Terrorantula's huge mechanical spider stomped on what undamaged police vehicles remained. On another monitor, I watched a live feed from Eyewitness 13's news van—at least until one of the huge mechanical spider legs impaled it. Then I had to switch to Newschannel 9.

Terrorantula tried to make his escape by climbing over city hall, but after the first two or three steps, the motors powering the legs began to whine. The cameraman from Newschannel 9 zoomed in to catch the worried look on Terrorantula's face as he turned to see Ultraviolet tugging the entire contraption backward by one of the legs.

"The power source to Terrorantula's vehicle should be located near the rear on the bottom of the body," I said into the microphone while I examined a diagnostic image of the machine from Phantom Ranger's files. "Or at least it was the last time he fought the Phantom Ranger. It should be easy to access the panel—"

Ultraviolet gave the leg a quick upward jerk and snapped it off the body, leaving some sparking wires and spinning gears.

"Or you could just do that," I added.

In rapid fire, she snapped off another leg and then another. After five, Terrorantula opened the cockpit to the vehicle with his hands raised in surrender.

"Whoa! Whoa!" he shouted. "What's with you super-heroes and breaking the legs off this thing? You think it's cheap to build a highly advanced piece of machinery like this? It's going to be more expensive to fix these legs than this thing is worth." He held up the piece of paper he'd tucked into his belt earlier, offering to hand it over to Ultraviolet in surrender.

"Get to class, Nate," Ultraviolet ordered, and as much as I wanted to know what was on that paper, I wanted even more not to get yelled at by Coach Howard.

28.6 Seconds

"Twenty-nine seconds. I think that's a new record," Coach Howard announced, waving his stopwatch above his head. "Way to go, McCaskill!"

Meathead McCaskill was bigger, faster, and stronger than anyone else in our gym class, which made him Coach's favorite student. He was the only teacher who felt that way, though. The reason Meathead was so big, fast, and strong was that he was three years older than everyone else in the class. Meathead had been held back so many times, he was the only eighth grader who kept shaving cream and a razor in his locker.

"And last but not least . . ." Coach looked at his clipboard. A snarl twisted his lips as he looked back down the obstacle course track and saw me and Teddy. "I take that back. Last *and* least, Banks and Cochrane!"

If Meathead was Coach's favorite player, Teddy and I

were neck and neck in the race to be his least favorite. I'd never seen much point in running unless someone was chasing me, and Teddy's P.E. career had been all downhill since he'd managed to break four toes during our fourth-grade square dancing unit—and only one of them had been his own.

The obstacle course was a long dirt path beyond the football field. Along it, Coach had laid out old tires, erected two splintery wooden walls with frayed ropes, rolled in two concrete pipes, and tossed out some old rusty metal hurdles. After the old Ditko Middle School had been destroyed, it had been rebuilt from the ground up with the promise of state-of-the-art facilities. The gymnasium was particularly impressive.

Or so I'd been told. I hadn't actually seen it yet.

Our old gym, which was also our cafeteria, auditorium, and site for the agriculture club to show off livestock twice a year, smelled like . . . well, like all four of those things rolled into one. Sort of a gym-socks-fish-sticks-burned-out-spotlight-cow-and-sheep kind of stink. The basketball hoops didn't come down from the ceilings all the way, so even the best players rarely could make a basket, since most shots ricocheted off the hoops at weird angles and bounced into the rafters. The volleyball net didn't fit into the holes in the floor correctly, so someone always had to hold each of its legs. And the old wrestling mats were more duct tape than mat.

The new gym was nicer than the basketball arena at the university, according to Fiona. Her gym class had been playing badminton there for weeks, and she couldn't say enough wonderful things about the new space.

But Coach Howard refused to let any of his classes near the new gym. For that matter, he refused to let us play on the new football field or run on the new track. Fiona and her girls class, on the other hand, had done an obstacle course similar to ours using lightweight canvas tunnels and fiberglass hurdles and a rock climbing wall.

It didn't make much sense, but then I remembered that Coach Howard seemed truly to enjoy making his students miserable.

"Let's go, ladies!" Coach shouted.

I exploded off the starting line and into the tires the coach had laid out on the dirt path. I had grown accustomed to reacting quickly when Keystone shouted orders at me during our training sessions. The tires could have easily tripped me up if not for the two months I'd spent jumping from one stone pillar to another in Keystone's cave. The centers of the tires were larger than the pillars—and they weren't covered in slippery green moss—so breezing through was no challenge at all.

Next was a wall with a rope to climb. During the second week of my training, I'd struggled to climb a rope in Keystone's cavern. Then he began tossing lit firecrackers at the floor beneath my feet. Naturally, I became a much better rope climber. The wall next to Coach Howard's rope made the climb infinitely easier, and I was over the top in no time.

After that, I hit the dirt and crawled through a fifteen-foot-long concrete pipe, using a technique I'd learned for staying low and moving quickly while patrolling the rooftops of Kurtzburg with Keystone at night.

Finally, the coach had set up two hurdles just before the finish line. While all the other kids had leapt over them one at a time, I quickly estimated they were no farther apart than the roof of the Malve Industries warehouse in Kurtzburg's wharf district and the fire escape of the building next door. I'd made that jump five times just a week earlier.

I launched myself over the first hurdle. It took only a fraction of a second to realize that while I might have estimated the distance correctly, I'd failed to consider the height of the hurdle. There was no way I'd be able to land on my feet without slamming my knees into the hurdle.

Instead, I shifted my weight in the air, diving forward so the hurdle brushed against my stomach.

I tucked my shoulder and rolled across the finish line, using a move I'd learned early in my training. Learning to fall without injuring myself just might have been the skill I relied on most.

Coach Howard hit the button on his stopwatch but didn't glance at the time. He just stared at me, his mouth wide open in shock. I quickly realized that everyone else was doing the same thing.

"How did I do?" I asked. He seemed to snap back to the job at hand.

"Twenty . . ." He took a deep breath and reluctantly read, "Twenty-eight point six."

Some of my classmates let out a short, excited cheer while the rest murmured their surprise to one another. Meathead narrowed his eyes, but I didn't worry about him. Instead, I turned to accept a congratulatory high five from Teddy only to find he wasn't at my side.

Looking back down the course, I spotted him at the rope wall. I watched as his foot slipped off the wall, leaving him to dangle from the rope and crash into the wooden planks. "Am I allowed to get a boost?" he called to Coach Howard.

"Just go around it, Cochrane!" Coach barked.

Teddy hustled around the wall, eventually emerged from the pipe, and caught each of the hurdles with the toes of his right foot as he tried to clear them.

"DQ," Coach said.

"Dairy Queen?" Teddy responded with a puzzled expression.

"Disqualified!" Coach roared. "You have to finish in less than two minutes. You're never going to make it."

Teddy shrugged and joined the rest of us well behind the finish line. I felt bad for him, but he didn't seem bothered by the outcome.

"I thought we were getting ice cream," he mumbled quietly.

More Than a Million...
for a Comic Book?

I was jumpy for the rest of the school day. I was certain there would be another supervillain attack. The slightest movement I saw out of the corner of my eye might be Antisocialite bursting into my math class. Footsteps in the hallway were probably those of a student going to the nurse's office, but they could have been Sawhorse making his way toward the cafeteria to attack a bunch of sixth graders.

When the final bell rang, I was almost more surprised by the lack of another incident than I had been by either Screamfang's or Terrorantula's attack. With every step of our walk from school to Funny Pages, our local comic-book store, I anticipated the frantic buzzing of the monitor. Every Friday, my friends and I went to Funny Pages to pick up the newest releases, but all of us seemed to have other things on our minds today.

"Did you ever find out what Terrorantula was doing at the mayor's mansion?" Fiona asked.

I checked the crisis monitor for an update. "It says here that he broke into a safe in the mayor's bedroom to steal the deed to DeFalco Mansion."

"The deed?" Teddy repeated. "What's he going to do with that?"

"Maybe he thought he could sell it."

"That makes no sense," Fiona argued.

"We're talking about a guy who builds robotic spiders and uses them to commit crimes all around the world," I noted. "You're surprised he did something that doesn't make sense? If you're going to be a superhero, you'd better get used to it."

Fiona's hand went to the Ring of Mercury on the chain around her neck. "Let's not talk about that," she said, dismissing me, which she seemed to do whenever the topic of being a superhero came up. "Did you check to see what books are coming out this week?" She didn't say anything else for the rest of the walk to the store, but that was okay, since Teddy didn't stop talking the entire time.

"Kind of a light week," Teddy started. "That's good, because I need to save up for Kanigher Kon." He went on to recall many of the exclusive action figures, comics, and collectibles that he was hoping to pick up at the convention. "I still have some Christmas money left over, so if there's that booth selling those Man-Ghost bobbleheads from last year, I should have enough this time."

Funny Pages was a small store that felt even tinier because of the maze of tables Jeff, the owner, had winding through the place. Each table was covered in box after box of old comic books. The tables bowed in the middle from the weight of the comics and looked like they were about to snap in half.

Some of the regular customers were peppered throughout the store. We didn't know any of their real names. They went by nicknames they'd made up to insult one another, like Blubbs, Stench, and 20 Questions.

"Did you see the big news yet?" Blubbs yelled before we were even in the door. "There was a fire at Don Neagle's penthouse."

"The computer guy?" Teddy asked.

"Computer guy?" Stench scoffed. "Don Neagle is a technology mogul. Do you have any idea how many things you use every day that Don Neagle helped either create or improve?" He crossed his arms and glared at Teddy.

"Uh . . . no?" Teddy replied.

"Of course you don't! None of us do! Don Neagle himself probably doesn't know. That's how much he's done."

"What does this have to do with a fire?" Fiona interrupted, stepping between Teddy and Stench.

"Don Neagle is one of the world's biggest comic-book collectors," Blubbs explained. "The fire was sparked by a wiring problem in the vault where he keeps his collection."

"Doesn't he have sprinklers or something?" Fiona asked.

"No, not sprinklers," Stench said. "You don't want to spray water on your comics."

"There's some kind of system that sucks all the oxygen out of the room," Blubbs went on. "But before it could do its job, a dozen or so of his books were burned, including . . ." He paused for drama. *"Outlandish Odysseys* number nineteen."

"No way," I gasped in shock. *Outlandish Odysseys* #19 was published in 1938 and featured the very first appearance of Man-Ghost. There were only five copies left in the entire world. "That thing's worth eight hundred thousand dollars."

"More," Blubbs said, correcting me. "Last year a copy sold for eight hundred thousand, but Neagle's copy was in better shape. It was probably worth more than a million."

"For a comic?" Teddy asked in disbelief.

This was why I took such good care of my comics. I never bought a new comic book unless it was flawless, without any scuff marks or tiny creases on the cover.

When I was done reading them, I put each one in a plastic sleeve with an acid-free piece of cardboard to keep it protected from moisture, air, and bending. The better shape the comic was in, the more it was worth.

Teddy, on the other hand, was never as careful with his comics. At his house, he'd leave them spread across his bedroom floor or on the back of the toilet. That was why he always was the first one to the checkout counter.

Jeff had his head down, looking over some paperwork. It took him a moment even to notice Teddy waiting with his money out.

"Oh, sorry about that, Teddy," he said. "Landlord sent me a new lease for the next year." He picked up just one comic and rang it into the register. "Is that it? Did you see there's an *Astro, Kid Genius Quarterly* out this week?"

"I saw, but I'm trying to save up my money for Kanigher Kon."

"Seems like everybody's trying to save money lately," Jeff said with a sad sigh. "Rent on the shop is going up, but sales are going down. I don't know what I'm going to do."

"Too bad you don't have some old comic you can sell for a million dollars," Teddy said.

"Unfortunately, I have plenty of old comics. Look at all these boxes." Jeff threw out his arms at the tables and tables of old comic boxes. "I have all these, plus some in my mom's garage, and more in a storage locker. But do you have any idea how long it's been since anyone came in here looking for a copy of—"

He reached into one of the boxes at random, pulled out a comic, and read the cover.

"*Hammer and Sickle Xtreme Team* number four?" His shoulders slumped and he let out a long sigh.

"Well, that's a bad example," Stench laughed. "Nobody bought that when it was new, either."

"Hey, I have a copy of that," Teddy protested. "Or at least I used to until I spilled orange juice on it a few years ago."

In fact, we'd both bought our copies at the same time, because Jeff had convinced us to pick them up years earlier, when we were first starting our comic-book collections. Now I knew why. No one but a gullible six-year-old would even think about reading that garbage.

Hammer and Sickle was a comic from the 1960s about two Russian superheroes. But in the 1990s, some comic publisher updated it to make it cooler and more modern. The result was a comic about Russian superheroes who had mullets, wore ugly costumes and big sunglasses, and were always gritting their teeth.

The new artist didn't seem to understand human anatomy, either. Hammer's and Sickle's thighs were the size of small cars, but their feet were tiny nose-sized triangles. Their shoulders were as wide as pool tables, but their waists looked more like pool cues. If he didn't know how to draw something, he would hide it. That meant characters often hung out in smoky rooms so he didn't have to draw their feet, and everyone wore wristbands so he didn't have to draw wrists. Worst of all, there were muscles everywhere. I don't know if it's physically possible to have muscular elbows, but Hammer and Sickle did.

"They printed a couple hundred thousand copies of this issue," Jeff recalled. "I think maybe a few hundred sold. If you look on the Internet, you can find people selling two hundred copies for a dollar. I know I have at least a thousand in my mom's garage."

"Too bad you can't sell those for half a million dollars," Teddy said.

"Yeah," Jeff said with a chuckle. "If only."

Jeff stared at the comic for a few minutes in a way that made me uncomfortable interrupting him to pay for my comics. He broke his longing gaze to ring us up, but then went back to deeply contemplating the old comic.

As we walked out the door, I glanced back to see him still staring intently at the comic, a weird grin on his face.

This Place Is
a Zoo

I didn't think the fire was nearly as important as Blubbs
and the rest of the crowd at Funny Pages did. It got only
a brief mention on that evening's local newscast, and no
one even commented about it on the comic blogs I read.

"A fire in the Darwyn City apartment of philanthropist
Don Neagle caused only minor damage," the anchorman
said to the camera. "Neagle was not home at the time
of the incident, and fire safety systems extinguished the
flames before they could spread to other apartments."

"Well, that's good news," his bubbly blond co-anchor
chimed in.

"Did she just say it was good news that someone's
apartment caught on fire?" my dad said, looking up from
the chicken he was chopping up for dinner.

"I think she meant it was good news that no one else's
apartment burned up," I offered.

"I get it," Dad said. "But I know if our house burned down and someone said it was good news that it didn't spread to the neighbors', I'd be a little upset."

"The house might go up in flames if you don't turn down the stove," Mom said as she came in from the garage. She turned the knobs to lower the flames beneath the empty pan in which Dad would be making chicken tacos. "You're going to ruin the pan. Again."

She pecked my dad on the cheek, and I turned back to the TV. The anchors had moved on to the next story, which featured clips of a panda eating some green branches.

"Kanigher Falls' newest visitor is settling in at her new home. Shu Fang, a four-year-old panda on loan from the Chuhing Zoo in China, is one of only a handful of pandas residing in North America."

"We should go do that tomorrow," Dad piped up.

"Do what?" I asked.

"Go see the panda," he replied. "Remember last June I paid for a yearlong family pass to the zoo? And how many times have we gone? Once."

"And I think we all remember why we only went once," Denise reminded him, looking up from her homework.

It had been 110 degrees out the day we'd bought the pass, and it had only gotten hotter as the summer went on. If the Arizona summers weren't overwhelming enough on their own, just imagine the smell of the monkey cages in that heat.

"It's February," Dad argued. "It'll be a fun family thing. Your mom has the day off. Besides, when was the last time we did something fun as a family?"

I locked eyes with Denise. The last time we'd done anything as a family had been the week before Christmas. Dad got some discounted tickets to *The Nutcracker* and decided we'd all benefit from soaking up the culture of the ballet.

Instead, Denise had tripped me while we were going down the steps to our seats, and I got her back by pouring a dozen or so warm, melty Milk Duds into her purse during intermission. She discovered them in the middle of the "Dance of the Sugar Plum Fairy" and screamed at me so loudly that one of the dancers fell down.

There was a reason we didn't do "fun family things" very often. But that never seemed to stop my dad from trying.

o o o

As soon as we entered the zoo, everyone around us turned to the right, ignoring the nocturnal predators exhibit to the left and the re-creation of an African savannah straight ahead. Nobody so much as slowed his pace as he passed the orangutans, gorillas, and chimpanzees in the primates pavilion. Thousands of people had turned out for one reason only—to see Shu Fang the panda.

"This is crazy, Dad," Denise complained as we made our way through the throngs of people. "Can we go home?"

Mom agreed. "The panda is going to be here for six months," she reminded my father. "Why don't we come back some other time when it isn't so crowded?"

"We're almost there," Dad assured us, standing on his tiptoes to see over the crowd. "It's right up there. Nate, try going to the left. The crowd's a little thinner over there."

I worked my way between people who all had the same thought my dad did. Eventually, I reached the railing of the rhinoceros habitat and could go no farther.

Dad shrugged. "Well, I guess now we wait."

"Shu Fang is one of fewer than three thousand pandas in existence," a recorded voice announced.

After five minutes, we'd gotten only about four inches closer to Shu Fang. Denise renewed her request to leave, but by now the crowd behind us was as thick as the crowd in front of us.

"The panda is an omnivore, though its diet consists

almost entirely of bamboo," the recorded voice continued. "An adult panda can eat as much as thirty pounds of bamboo every day."

I climbed up the rhino railing to get a better view of what lay ahead. Denise gave me a shove, and I spun around, steadying myself by gripping the rail.

"Very funny!" I yelled. "Do you want me to fall in with the rhinoceros?" It was about a twelve-foot drop from the railing to the pit where the rhinos lived.

But Denise hadn't pushed me to be mean. The person behind her had pushed her into me, and that was because the person behind him had been pushed. In fact, from my higher vantage point, I could see the crowd rippling forward as bodies slammed into one another.

In my pocket, I felt the familiar vibration of the crisis monitor I carried at all times. Turning back toward the zoo entrance, I saw a man whose head rose above the rest of the crowd. His shoulders were as wide as two men standing side by side. He wore a black suit coat, a red-striped tie, and a tiny black cap. I couldn't see his legs, but I knew he was wearing short pants.

"Schoolboy Krush," I muttered.

"Hey, quit pushing," someone nearby shouted as another wave of Schoolboy's progress rippled through the crowd. The giant of a man was moving people aside with sweeps of his massive arms, as though he was swimming through the crowd toward the panda.

I reached one hand into my pocket to pull out the crisis monitor. The small video screen showed a map of Kanigher Falls with a red dot flashing over the zoo.

"No, really?" I grumbled sarcastically to myself.

Because I was staring at the screen, I didn't notice when the next wave of shoving came through. Denise's shoulder collided with my thigh, knocking me off balance. My left foot slipped off the railing and I toppled backward into the rhino pit. Instinctively, my arm shot out to grab the railing, letting loose my grip on the crisis monitor. It tumbled into a mud puddle below with a squishy plop.

"Development in China has wiped out most of the panda's natural lowland habitat," the voice informed the now panicking crowd.

I gripped the bottom railing with both hands, letting my legs swing around so that the rest of my body slammed into the sloped wall of the rhino enclosure. I heard my dad shout my name, but I was focusing on the crisis monitor in the mud beneath me. Pulling myself up would have been easy, but I didn't want to have to explain to Keystone that I'd lost my monitor. Plus if Ultraviolet needed my help, the monitor could be our only way to communicate.

With a deep, reluctant breath, I let go of the railing and slid down the rough, steep incline as my dad shouted after me. My feet hit the muck and each slipped in a different direction, which meant that I was soon waist deep in mud. At least, I hoped that was what it was.

I grabbed the crisis monitor and wiped a thick layer of mud from its screen.

"Nate!" my mom shouted. "Sit tight! We'll get you out of there."

"Forget that," Denise yelled. "Run, you idiot!"

Early in my training, Keystone had taught me the two most important rules of success as a superhero: Be aware of your surroundings, and don't do anything stupid. And I had broken both rules.

I looked up from the crisis monitor's readout to find myself nose to nose with the horn of a rhinoceros. He did not look happy to see me.

Rhinos Don't Bite

Everything is about perspective. When Meathead McCaskill corners you in the cafeteria and demands your lunch money, you can't help feeling intimidated. But compare that to staring down a five-thousand-pound rhinoceros and it's nothing. And while that rhino might have seemed like a pretty scary proposition, I'd been held hostage by a nuclear-powered science teacher, nearly frozen to death in a sauerkraut-flavored avalanche, and sealed in a gas-filled room by a Cold War–era Soviet madman, so compared to those things—

Well, actually, the rhinoceros was still pretty scary.

"Good news!" my sister yelled down to me. "It says on this sign that rhinos don't have teeth in the front of their mouths for biting."

Being bitten was the last thing I was worried about.

I was concentrating entirely on that three-foot-long horn pointing directly at my face.

"Oh, and they're herbivores, Nate."

"Denise, you're not helping," my mom scolded her.

The rhino hadn't moved since I had spotted him, and neither had I. I remembered a little factoid I'd heard or read somewhere: A rhino's vision is based on motion. So if I didn't move, he couldn't see me.

Then I remembered that was true of a tyrannosaurus, not a rhinoceros.

"Nate," my dad whispered loudly. "Grab my jacket."

Without moving a muscle, I shifted my eyes as far to my left as I could. At the very edge of my peripheral vision, my dad's jacket hung against the side of the enclosure like the rope against Coach Howard's obstacle course wall.

But as long as I didn't move, the rhino didn't, either. With each passing second, I felt a little bit safer. I was pretty sure that as long as nothing startled him, I wouldn't get hurt.

That was when the sirens sounded.

I would later learn that the alarm had been triggered when Schoolboy Krush leapt into the panda habitat. When I heard that, I couldn't help wondering why no one had seemed to care when I fell into the rhino pit.

But at the moment, I wasn't wondering why the sirens were going off. I was just concerned with the effect they were having on the two-and-a-half-ton beast in front of me. When he heard the alarm, he jerked his head toward the sound and let out an angry snort of surprise.

In one motion, I shoved the crisis monitor into my mouth and spun to grab the jacket. My dad was lying on his stomach with one arm wrapped around the bottom rung of the railing and the other holding an arm of the jacket.

"Hurry, Nate!" he shouted.

In no time, I flew up the jacket and gripped my dad's wrist. Even without looking back, I could feel the massive presence of the rhinoceros lunging toward me. I snatched hold of the railing, over which my mom reached to help pull me up, but I didn't need any assistance. It's not difficult to find motivation when you're trying to get away from a monster nearly fifty times your size.

Once I no longer needed both hands free, I took the monitor from my mouth, then spit a large glob of mud back into the rhino's pit. At least, I hoped it was mud. I quickly slid the monitor back into my pocket before my parents could see it.

Dad slid out from under the barrier and got to his feet. "The good news is there's no crowd to see the panda now," he joked over the screams of zoo visitors and the wail of the panda siren.

Mom glared at him. I had a feeling we wouldn't be doing any more "fun family things" for a while. She pulled me close and started to poke at me to make sure I wasn't hurt. Mom is an emergency-room surgeon, but she saved cool, calm demeanor and bedside manner for her real patients.

"Mom, I'm fine," I insisted as I tried to pull my head away. She gripped my jaw and stared into my eyes. I knew from previous encounters that she was checking for signs of a concussion.

"What's your name?" she asked slowly.

"Nathan Banks," I replied. "And I'm at the zoo and it's Saturday." I was already familiar with the questions she would ask next.

"And who am I?" she asked, prodding me.

"He just said, '*Mom,* I'm fine,'" Denise interrupted. "*They* aren't." She pointed toward a dozen or so people lying on the ground, each clinging to various body parts. Whether they'd been tossed aside by Schoolboy's massive arms or trampled by the fleeing crowd, it was clear they needed help.

It was as if someone had just removed a blindfold from my mom's eyes. She hurriedly made her way from person to person, assessing their injuries and doing what she could until the paramedics arrived.

Meanwhile, I drifted over to the panda exhibit. Inside, Schoolboy Krush was struggling to remove the panda. According to the recorded voice, which continued to play over the alarm, the panda weighed 290 pounds. That shouldn't have posed much of a challenge for Schoolboy. Then again, there's a difference between picking up a 290-pound barbell and picking up a 290-pound creature with sharp teeth and claws that really doesn't want to be picked up.

"Ouch, would you—Don't do that!" Schoolboy shouted as he tried to hold Shu Fang's mouth shut with one hand while hefting her onto his shoulder with the other. "Stop squirming, you stupid bear!"

He changed strategy, attempting to pin the panda's arms to her sides and carry her off tucked up into his armpit. He hadn't made much progress with that technique before Ultraviolet showed up.

As she descended from the sky, Ultraviolet shifted her focus briefly from Schoolboy Krush to me, giving a confused shrug, as if asking why I was there. Mud still clogged the microphone and speaker of my monitor, which prevented me from communicating with her. I tried to yell over the sirens, the shouts of zoo visitors, and Shu Fang's squeals, but quickly resorted to hand gestures instead.

I pointed at Schoolboy with one hand and then at the top of my head with the other. "HIS! HAT! HIS! HAT!"

If I'd had the time to discuss his background in detail, I would have explained that Schoolboy Krush derived his incredible strength from his hat. He didn't dress like a boarding school fourth grader for fashion's sake.

Schoolboy dropped Shu Fang and picked up a rock the size of a desk, leaving a crater in the middle of the grassy hill where the panda lounged. Schoolboy hurled the rock at Ultraviolet, who caught it as easily as if it were a beach ball.

Meanwhile, Shu Fang calmly gnawed a stalk of bamboo.

While Ultraviolet gently lowered the rock, Schoolboy Krush charged her and uncorked a superpowered shoulder tackle to her midsection. The force of the impact threw them both into the cement side wall of the enclosure.

With his arms still wrapped around Ultraviolet's waist, Schoolboy reared back. It looked as though he was about to drive Ultraviolet into the now cracked wall of the panda's home.

But he was in for a surprise.

Ultraviolet flew into the sky with Schoolboy still holding on to her waist, only now he was holding on to save his own life rather than to crush hers. She flew higher and higher until they weren't much more than a dot against the blue sky.

Police swarmed the area wearing body armor, and some carried riot shields. They spotted Ultraviolet in the sky and gave a signal to the paramedics that it was okay to move in.

Mom began rattling off diagnoses for the injured people on the ground. While the paramedics tended to the victims, Ultraviolet swooped back down and dropped Schoolboy to the ground at the feet of some police officers. He no longer wore his cap and he seemed to be shrinking, though he still wasn't what anyone would describe as "small."

Ultraviolet tossed his hat to a woman I recognized.

Detective Hemm had once threatened to arrest me when I called the police to report a kidnapping by Coldsnap, a supervillain who'd buried Kanigher Falls in snow. It seemed I wasn't the only one to recognize the short, disheveled police detective.

"Maylin?" Schoolboy Krush gasped. "You're a cop now?"

They Make Great Pets

"Put him in a patrol car," Detective Hemm ordered two officers as she examined Schoolboy's cap.

"Of all the people I never thought I'd see again—" Schoolboy said to Detective Hemm with a laugh as the police dragged him to a patrol car.

Detective Hemm dropped the hat into a plastic bag marked EVIDENCE. "Would you care to make a statement, Ms. Ultraviolet?" she asked.

"This guy was trying to steal the panda, so I stopped him," Ultraviolet replied. "I'm not sure what else I can tell you."

"Three supervillains in two days," Detective Hemm said, eying Ultraviolet suspiciously. "That's got to be a record."

"Considering the old record was two supervillains in forever, yeah," I piped up.

Detective Hemm shot a glance toward my dad, my sister, and me, noticing us for the first time. "Hey, you're that kid," she said.

"Be quiet, Nate," my dad said.

"What's the name again?" she muttered under her breath. "It's a money thing. Penny? No, that's a girl's name. Quarters. Dime. Nickel. Nichols? Is your last name Nichols?"

"Banks," Ultraviolet answered for me. "Nate Banks."

"What do you think, Nate Banks?" Detective Hemm asked me. "Any idea why Kanigher Falls is now Supervillain Central?" She cast her eyes suspiciously toward Ultraviolet. I couldn't tell whether she was accusing Ultraviolet of being a part of the attacks, or if she just didn't like superheroes.

"Why don't you ask Schoolboy?" I suggested. "He seemed willing to talk to you."

"Nate!" my dad barked. Denise was less subtle, punching me in the back.

"He has a point," Ultraviolet said.

"I suppose he does," Detective Hemm reluctantly agreed.

The two of them walked toward the squad cars and I followed. My dad reached out and grabbed me by my elbow.

"Where are you going?" he whispered harshly.

"I was going to go hear what they had to say," I replied.

"Are you crazy?" he snapped. "You need to sit down and relax. You almost died in that rhino pit because that idiot started a riot over—what?—a panda? It doesn't make any sense."

I couldn't remember ever seeing my dad so upset. When I'd nearly been trapped in a school bus that plummeted off the Moldoff Bridge, my mom had flipped out, but Dad had taken it in stride. I realized that this was the first time he'd personally seen me in the kind of danger that was becoming fairly routine for me.

"You're right, Dad," I said, consoling him, putting my hand on his shoulder. "It doesn't make sense. But it might make more sense if we heard what they were saying."

Dad's nervous expression melted away and he gave me a sly smile. Then he accompanied me as I inched closer to the squad car where Schoolboy was being held. He was stuffed into the backseat of the patrol car so tightly he resembled a Thanksgiving turkey in a toaster oven. Dad and I slipped behind a pillar next to the baboon enclosure and near the squad cars. We silently moved forward until we could hear most of the conversation.

"I had a feeling you'd be coming to talk to me, May," the supervillain said with a chuckle.

"What's with all the supervillain attacks in the Falls lately?" Detective Hemm growled.

"I'm sorry," he said with mock innocence. "I don't know what you're talking about. You don't—oh, no! You don't think *I'm* a supervillain, do you? I'm just an overly excited animal lover. I came here today to see the new panda and I fell into the enclosure by mistake. Ultraviolet, thank you so much for saving me."

"Can it, Schoolboy," Hemm snapped.

"Of course, *Officer*." He dragged out the last word and stared at Detective Hemm challengingly. "If I knew anything about supervillains, I'd certainly help you out. But then, you know a lot about supervillains already, don't you, May?"

Detective Hemm grunted.

Something suddenly seemed to dawn on Schoolboy.

"You know, now that you mention it, I might have heard something about some supervillains," he drawled. "Too bad I can't remember the details. It's probably because I'm so nervous about this misunderstanding with the panda. I've had a few run-ins with the law in my past, and this could look really bad on my record. Of course, you wouldn't know anything about having a criminal record, May, would you?"

"You will address me as Detective Hemm," she snapped.

"I apologize, *Detective*," Schoolboy replied, though he didn't sound sorry. "Maybe if I had a fine, upstanding, decorated officer of the law like yourself to support my story, I wouldn't be so worried about my record. I might remember whatever it was I heard about supervillains coming to Kanigher Falls."

Detective Hemm backed away and took a deep breath. I'm pretty sure she counted to ten before turning back to face Schoolboy. "I can put in a good word for you," she agreed. "That is, if you give me some valuable information. But if you're not straight with me . . . ," she threatened, her face twitching with rage.

I was standing twenty feet away with my dad's hand on my shoulder and Ultraviolet and at least four police officers between me and Schoolboy Krush, and still I was frightened of him. You would think that being half his size, Detective Hemm might have been intimidated, but instead it was Schoolboy who seemed to begin backing down.

"Okay, okay, just chill out, Maylin," he said.

"I told you, it's *Detective* Hemm," she insisted. "That is, unless you want me to start calling you Percival."

"Sorry. Detective Hemm." All the sarcasm left Schoolboy's voice. "I'll tell you what I know. A week or so ago,

I heard there was a special opportunity for enterprising people like myself."

"Go on," Detective Hemm said, pressing him.

"You promise you'll put in a good word for me?" Schoolboy asked.

"I promise that I'll put in a bad one if I don't have all the details in the next thirty seconds," she snapped back.

"Okay, okay," Schoolboy agreed. "There's a nice fat payday out there for whoever pulls off the biggest heist in Kanigher Falls. Plus there's a little extra in it if that person can also embarrass *her*." He pointed at Ultraviolet.

This made Ultraviolet's mouth fall open in surprise, which was no easy task. As Ms. Matthews, she had once asked where the Korean War was fought and hadn't even flinched when Teddy had answered, "Vietnam." It was hard to rattle her, but Schoolboy had managed to do it.

Hemm continued the interrogation. "Why her?"

Schoolboy looked back at Detective Hemm like she'd asked a stupid question. "Come on, May—I mean, *Detective*. Nobody told me that. And I didn't ask. I hear there's money to be made embarrassing some new-kid-on-the-block superhero, I don't care who wants it done or why. I only care that the cash is good."

"So why the zoo?"

"Do you know what a panda bear goes for on the black market? Why bother with security at a bank when that thing is worth at least a million dollars and it's just sitting out in the open eating tree branches?"

"A million dollars?" I gasped.

Schoolboy, Detective Hemm, and Ultraviolet turned to look at us, and I felt my dad's grip tighten on my shoulder.

"What?" Schoolboy barked at me. "They're nearly extinct or something, and the rarer something is, the more it's worth. What do you want me to do? Rob a jewelry store? Boring."

He turned his attention back to Ultraviolet. "Plus I thought if she got involved, I could get on the news hitting her over the head with an elephant or something. That would make for some good TV. Better than the coverage Terrorantula got. I don't know what he was thinking."

"Who else has heard about this deal?" Ultraviolet asked.

"There was a meeting with a dozen or so of us, but a lot of the others are already in jail, and you know how word gets around," he answered. "Who can say? Anyone who thinks they're tough enough might take a shot at you now." He gave Detective Hemm a wicked grin, and she responded by slamming the door hard enough to rock the car violently.

"Get him down to booking!" she shouted at another officer, who jumped into the car and took off. "Bad enough we still have those other two yahoos down there. You'd think that would get the SDD here faster, but no such luck."

The SDD was the Superhuman Detention Division, a federal agency that oversees the special prisons needed to lock up guys who could knock down cinder block walls with their pinkie fingers or slide between iron bars like rubber. "Guess I'd better call them so they can start processing Schoolboy or I'll be stuck with all three of them until Monday." She took her cell phone out of her pocket and started to dial.

"Do you need me for anything else?" Ultraviolet asked.

"Not right now," Detective Hemm said while she waited for someone to answer her call. "But if what Krush told us is true, I have a bad feeling we'll be seeing each other again soon."

Big Bucks for
Mint Condition

I spent the next day trying not to think much about the three supervillains who'd attacked my hometown, but I was doing a lousy job of it. I tried reading comic books, but if there's one thing that won't take your mind off supervillains, it's reading a bunch of stories about supervillains.

I was lying on the bed, flipping through the newest issue of *Hurricane Squad,* when the doorbell rang. I heard the door open and my mom talking to someone, but I couldn't make out the words. I figured it was probably someone selling something or offering to trim the trees in the yard, so I went back to my comic.

A moment later, my mom called for me. "Nate, you have a visitor."

Teddy was spending the afternoon at the mall with Allison Heaton, his girlfriend, who was in seventh grade, and Fiona spent Sundays at her dad's house, so I wasn't expecting anyone to drop by. I went out of my room and started down the stairs.

I could see a man waiting for me on the other side of the screen door. I immediately got defensive. My mind had been preoccupied with supervillains, and for a moment I wondered if some superpowered baddie planned to get to Ultraviolet through me. After all, it had happened before.

"Hey, Nate," the man said. "Sorry to bother you, but I was passing by on my way to work. I need to ask you a question that can't wait until next Friday."

"Jeff?" I barely recognized the comic-book store owner. I couldn't remember the last time I'd seen him out from behind the counter. Without the pale fluorescent lighting and the dingy beige walls covered in comics and posters, he just didn't look the same.

"Um, how's it going?" I asked.

"I was wondering if you still have that run of *Hammer and Sickle Xtreme Team* you bought from me years ago."

"Yeah, of course," I answered.

"That's good. I know you take good care of your comics. What kind of shape is your copy of number four in?"

"Decent, I suppose."

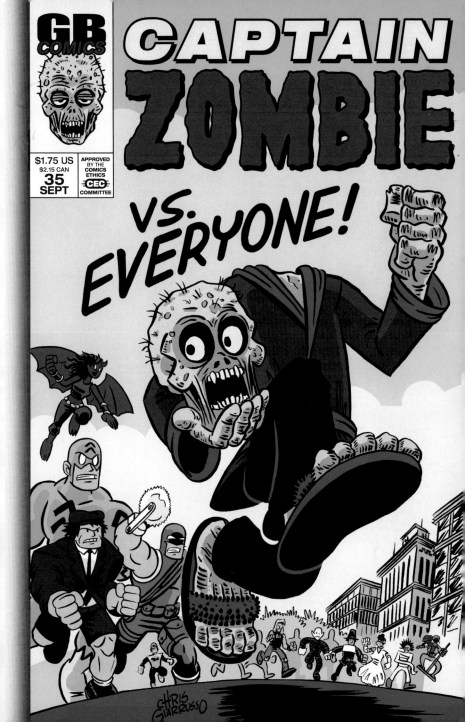

MONGOLIAN BEEF WITH A SIDE OF SUPERVILLAINS

WRITTEN BY **JAKE BELL**   ILLUSTRATED BY **CHRIS GIARRUSSO**

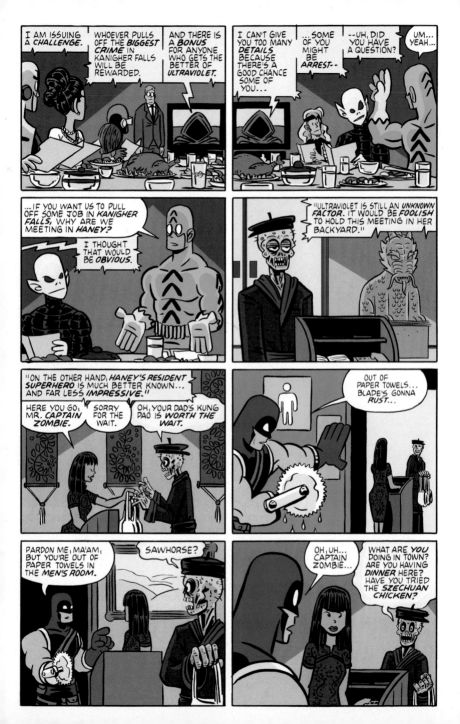

"Do you mind if I see it?"

I shrugged and asked him to wait in the living room while I ran upstairs. *Hammer and Sickle Xtreme Team* was filed under *H,* which was in the boxes under all my comics beginning with *D* through *G.* I heaved boxes aside until I had access to the issue Jeff wanted. He waited for me by the front door, talking on his cell phone.

"Let me look it up, but I think we can still get the shipment here in time if we go with the freight option. That'll be half the cost." He looked up and saw me. "I'll give you a call when I get into the store, okay? All right, thanks for getting back to me. Bye."

He closed the phone and turned his attention to the comic.

"Beautiful," Jeff remarked, his eyes lighting up. "Absolutely flawless. This is exactly what I need."

His phone rang. It blasted the music from the old *Marauder* TV series. He apologized and answered it.

"No, Blubbs, I need you to talk to every blogger you know. Put out the word everywhere. Fine, I'll double the price, but I need it done by Friday. Look, can I call you back?"

He hung up and turned his attention back to me.

"Sorry about that. Trying to arrange something

special for the convention. Now, as I was saying, this is just what I need."

I was confused. "What do you need that for? I thought you had thousands of those in your mom's garage."

"Yes, but a garage isn't the best place to store comic books. All the comics I've got out there are yellowing. Plus, to save space, I crammed as many into each box as I could, so a lot of them are wrinkled or torn."

His phone rang again. This time it played the theme song from the *Nightowl* animated series.

"Hey, dude, you got my message? Cool. Yeah, I know it's kind of a rush job, but we have a convention coming up next Friday. Uh-huh. Okay, well, if you can get on that, I'll send you my shipping account number tonight and they can just bill me. Thanks, man!"

He hung up and turned back to me.

"I have a special client in mind, and I don't want to waste his time with anything less than mint condition."

I couldn't imagine any serious collector being interested in *Hammer and Sickle Xtreme Team* #4, and I couldn't imagine anyone who'd buy a copy of *Hammer and Sickle Xtreme Team* #4 caring about finding a mint-condition copy.

"How about I give you"—he closed one eye and examined the comic from all angles again—"six dollars?"

I had paid two when I'd bought it years earlier, so tripling my investment on a worthless comic sounded like a great deal. It was even better since I knew I could buy two hundred copies of that issue for a dollar on eBay. We shook on it, I pocketed the cash, and Jeff carefully placed the comic book into a padded, reinforced envelope. He thanked me again and headed to work.

Six bucks! Not bad for a Sunday afternoon spent reading comic books. I could put that toward the con-exclusive Red Terra action figure I'd read about on my favorite comic blog. Kanigher Kon was going to have only one hundred of them.

After two rough days, Sunday was shaping up to be pretty great.

Then I felt that familiar vibration in my pocket.

As quickly as I could while still looking calm, I headed into the kitchen. My mom was busy making dinner.

"What was the comic-book guy here for?" she asked.

"Oh, he wanted me to sell him a comic book from my collection," I told her. "I'm going to go out for a little while, maybe walk around the neighborhood or something."

"Okay," she said. "Dinner should be in . . ." Her voice trailed off as she studied the ham she was preparing. "I don't really know how long it will be."

"All right," I replied, barely listening.

"Your dad tore the label off this ham, so I don't know how much it weighs."

"Uh-huh." I inched closer to the door, putting my hand on the knob.

"I looked it up in a cookbook," she went on. "It said twenty minutes per pound, but since I don't have the label . . ."

"Okay, Mom, talk to you later," I said, trying to get away. I twisted the doorknob and started to pull the door open.

"I mean, really," Mom said with a deep sigh. "Why would you tear off the label if you're not making it?"

"I don't know," I said. "If I see Dad, I'll ask him." I swung the door open and started out into the backyard.

"Two hours," she shouted after me. "Maybe more . . . or less!"

Jailbreak

I slipped through the backyard and into the alley where the garbage cans were. A few weeks earlier, a crew had installed what looked like a new gas main just outside our gate. I placed my palm on the fake regulator at the top and curled my fingers around it. Hidden sensors on the underside read my fingerprints and sent a signal to release the locks. The "gas main" split in two with a loud click and a hiss of rushing air to reveal a shaft similar to the elevators in Ultraviolet's and Keystone's lairs. The only difference was that this one was horizontal instead of vertical. Lying within the shaft was a pill-shaped craft, just large enough for me to fit into.

Keystone had wanted to build a secret tunnel directly from the closet in my bedroom to Ultraviolet's base of operations, but since my room is on the second floor, he had settled for this instead.

I lay on my back in the craft and watched the fake gas main close over me. A few seconds of whistling air was followed by a beeping countdown.

Then my body surged forward at a mind-numbing speed. The tunnel worked on the same principle as the elevators. A pneumatic tube shot the craft from the alley behind my house into the cave beneath the school like a bullet down the barrel of a gun. Keystone told me it was set to a top speed of sixty miles per hour, and that it could go faster, except the acceleration would probably kill me. As it was, I could be on duty at the monitoring station in less than thirty seconds.

The pod screeched to a stop and the craft cracked open with another hiss. I was ejected into the lair that had been secretly built beneath the school to serve as Ultraviolet's headquarters. I bolted upright and nearly fell over again. My head felt three times heavier than normal, because the sudden acceleration had pushed all the blood in my body into my brain.

I stumbled across the stone floor, holding on to the desks and anything else I could find that would support my weight. The lair was a natural cave that had been discovered when Ultraviolet and Dr. Malcontent fought each other in the skies over the building, eventually crashing through the school and the foundation below it. Keystone had hired a team of contractors to install the most advanced computer systems. The computers scanned nearly every stream of communication within one hundred miles for problems that might require Ultraviolet's assistance.

I sat in front of the monitors, my vision finally starting to clear. A red dot flashed over the main police station downtown. I tapped into the security cameras, but there was nothing to see. All the cameras were black. Someone had cut the feed.

I stuck the earpiece into my ear and tried to reach Ultraviolet. She responded, but her voice had the same tone as my mom's when I call her in the middle of an emergency room shift to ask if I can have some chips a half hour before dinner. The tone says: "I'm extremely busy here, so this better be important!"

"What do you have for me, Nate?" Ultraviolet asked.

"Nothing. All the cameras are out of commission. Backtracking to watch recorded video. Are you already there?"

"Yes, and there are escaped prisoners everywhere. Most are surrendering, but it's still chaos," she said.

I scrolled backward through the video until images finally replaced the blackness. Jail cells at the police station were open and empty. Police were scrambling. I couldn't make any sense of it, so I rewound further in the police station's security footage to a moment when everything had been less chaotic.

The video showed Screamfang, Terrorantula, and Schoolboy Krush in individual cells in the Kanigher Falls Police Station. I knew they were being held there until the Superhuman Detention Division got around to transferring them to a super-secure prison.

There was no audio, but it looked like the three of them were shouting to each other and laughing. Detective Hemm was on guard just outside the three cells. She didn't seem too amused by their jokes. Suddenly, she got up from her chair and stormed out of the cellblock. Moments later a black spot scurried across the floor and slipped through the bars of Schoolboy's cell. He knelt down and picked up what I could now see was his hat, but something remained on the floor. Two smaller spots scuttled into Terrorantula's cell.

"Spiderbots," I groaned.

The spiderbots had broken into the evidence locker and stolen Schoolboy's hat. I found the camera from the evidence room and rewound until I saw the bots creep into the room between the shoes of a woman in a rumpled suit.

Once Schoolboy had his cap squarely on his head, the bars to his cell might as well have been made of papier-mâché. He tore through them and then went to work on Screamfang's cell. Once free, Screamfang ran off while Schoolboy began pounding on the cinder block wall of his cell.

A few seconds later, Screamfang returned with keys. He sprung Terrorantula first, but then proceeded to unlock every cell in the station.

Why do they care about the other prisoners? I wondered.

Some of the inmates seemed reluctant to take part in the mass escape, but when someone the size of Schoolboy Krush wants you to see things his way, he can be quite influential. He tore open the hole in his cell until it was large enough for someone to run through to freedom.

Three police officers hurried into the room to find a flood of inmates pouring out onto the street. Screamfang opened his mouth and flattened the police officers with a scream that made a crack in the lens appear across the video image. The three supervillains hurried through the door the police had come through, heading back into the station and not out the hole in the wall.

"The supervillains aren't with the rest of the escapees," I announced into my earpiece microphone. "The regular prisoners are just a distraction." Ultraviolet didn't reply.

On the monitors, I watched the three supervillains break through a maintenance door and head into the basement of the station house.

And that was where the recording stopped, courtesy—I'd learn later—of a spiderbot that had been programmed to find and destroy all security measures in the building. Police later discovered that the villains had accessed the city sewers from the station house basement. Ultraviolet helped round up the escapees, but there was no way to track the three supervillains through the sewer. Something about the whole escape smelled funny, and it wasn't the sewer. Where had Detective Hemm gone just before the three supervillains had escaped? Had she had something to do with the plan?

The day before, Schoolboy had recognized her. I'd noticed at the time, but it hadn't made me suspicious until now. I figured she must have arrested Schoolboy in the past, but now I remembered how surprised he had been that she was a police officer. Had they known each other some other way?

Hoping it would turn up nothing, I typed HEMM, MAYLIN into a database search. Immediately, I had a biography and all sorts of unimportant information about her. She was the second of three children, all born in Rosandru. She played the saxophone. She had joined the police academy when she was in her late twenties. Everything looked innocent enough until I got to the end of the file. In red letters was a link that said LEGAL STATUS: PARDONED 05/2004.

I clicked on the link.

A similar page came up. Maylin Hemm was still the second of three children and still played the saxophone, but the page also included a file from the Superhuman Detention Division. Line after line had been scratched out with a black marker.

The only things that were still readable were a description of her powers and her former alias: Ms. Mayhem.

Mayhem

"I've got news," I told Teddy and Fiona as we biked to the cemetery. "Detective Maylin Hemm."

"What about her?" Fiona asked.

"I think she's a supervillain," I stated.

"No, she isn't," Teddy insisted. "She's a police officer."

"And she's a supervillain," I said. "May. Hemm."

"You're kidding me," Fiona moaned. "How did we not see this?"

"Considering we used to have a teacher named Mal Content, you would think we'd be better at noticing things like that," Teddy agreed as he leaned his bike against the willow tree.

"Did you tell Ultraviolet?" Fiona asked as we approached the Zuembay crypt.

"Sure, I told her," I said. "But Ms. Mayhem hasn't done anything illegal."

"Yet," Teddy added.

"I've never heard of Ms. Mayhem," Fiona said as she tore open the wrapper to a granola bar. "Who is she?"

"I guess when she was pardoned, a lot of her files were either destroyed or covered up," I explained. "What I read said she has superstrength and some level of invulnerability—"

"Like Ultraviolet," Teddy said.

"And half the other superheroes and supervillains out there," I noted. "She can't fly, though. And the file indicated something about problems with controlling her powers, but there weren't any details."

"Well, think positive," Teddy suggested. "Maybe she lost them."

"Maybe who lost what?" Captain Zombie asked. He was already pouring us sodas in crystal goblets that had the initials CZ etched into the glass.

"Have you ever heard of Ms. Mayhem?" Teddy asked him.

Captain Zombie's milky white eyes widened a bit and he took a deep breath. "Why? What happened?" he asked, doing a poor job of covering up his concern.

I began to tell him about the jailbreak. "On Saturday, she arrested Schoolboy Krush and seemed really on edge. But I figured that was because he kept—I don't know—teasing her, like he knew her, but not as a police officer. Then yesterday, Schoolboy and—" I stopped as a stray thought suddenly caught me.

On Thursday, Captain Zombie had had his head punched off by "one of the big bruisers" at the Chinese restaurant.

"You said Schoolboy Krush was at the Chinese restaurant last week, right?"

"Yeah," Captain Zombie said.

"What about Screamfang and Terrorantula?"

He thought for a second and nodded. "I know Screamfang was there. Terrorantula might have been there, too. There were a bunch of people in the back. Once my head came off, I kind of lost track of new faces."

"That must have been what Schoolboy was talking about," I declared, though no one in the room understood me. "Schoolboy said he'd been at a meeting with about a dozen supervillains last week. That must have been it." I looked determinedly into Captain Zombie's face. "What about Ms. Mayhem? Was she at the meeting?"

"No!" Captain Zombie insisted. "She doesn't live in Haney." He frowned and looked away. "And she's not Ms. Mayhem anymore."

"I read her file," I told Captain Zombie. "Almost

everything about Ms. Mayhem has been deleted. All it says is that she had trouble controlling her powers."

Captain Zombie swallowed hard and looked up for what seemed like forever at a corner where the ceiling met the wall. "Maylin Hemm," he began, but stopped.

"Maylin Hemm is not Ms. Mayhem," a strong voice behind us announced.

We all spun in surprise to see the Phantom Ranger standing on the marble stairs with Keystone just behind him.

"That's . . . that's the Phant—" Teddy whispered, his eyes wide with shock.

"Shhh," I said, cutting him off. Teddy had never met the Ranger, one of the most popular superheroes in the world, but Fiona and I had.

"What's going on down here?" Keystone barked. "We've been waiting for you up there for four minutes. Didn't I tell you to be on time?"

"Orpheus, chill," the Ranger said. "It's okay." The Ranger came down the last few steps to join us in the parlor.

"When Maylin Hemm developed her superpowers, she was just like you or me, or any other kid who wants to be a superhero," the Ranger told us. "Only, her powers didn't . . . come in quite right."

"What does that mean?" Fiona asked nervously.

"Remember what the Dart's been telling you?" Keystone asked, jumping in. "About how it's more important that you learn to control your speed than it is to go faster? All the power in the world is no good without control."

"And Maylin couldn't control her power," Captain Zombie added.

Her superstrength, they explained, became dangerous. She couldn't hug her mom without breaking ribs. She couldn't pet a puppy or she'd crush it. Everywhere she went, she left a path of destruction. Doors torn off hinges, windows shattered, cars flipped over, sidewalks and streets cracked.

And that was just a typical walk to the mailbox.

"And so she decided to become a supervillain," I concluded.

"No!" Captain Zombie almost shouted. "Think about it. A couple of police officers saw a teenage girl knocking down a brick wall. They didn't realize she had done it by mistake, and they told her to stop. She got scared and told them to leave her alone."

"Which they didn't," Phantom Ranger added.

"They tried to arrest her," Keystone recalled. "She snapped those handcuffs—they might as well have wrapped her wrists up in thread. She broke one cop's arm and the other one's leg—"

"All while trying not to hurt them," Captain Zombie reminded Keystone.

"Right," Phantom Ranger agreed. "But when something like that happens, even if it's an accident, the SDD moves pretty fast to declare you a supervillain. She didn't call herself Ms. Mayhem. When she finally was taken into custody, the person who phoned in the report to the SDD home office gave them her name: Ms. May Hemm."

"And the person on the other end wrote it 'Mayhem,'" I guessed.

The three all nodded.

"She seems to have it under control now," I noted.

"True, but it's not easy," Phantom Ranger said. "She spent two years in a superhuman detention facility—"

"That's probably why Schoolboy recognized her," Captain Zombie suggested.

"We managed to work with her, get her some training," the Ranger went on. "Still, all that did was allow her to control herself through absolute concentration. She can't afford to get distracted for more than a few seconds or people could die."

"So that's why she always seems so . . . ," I said, not

sure what word I should use with these three men, who obviously respected Detective Hemm quite a bit.

"Mean?" Captain Zombie offered.

"Yeah."

"If she has to decide between hurting your feelings or breaking every bone in your body, which would you have her choose?" Phantom Ranger asked with a laugh.

"She has to constantly struggle not to lose concentration," Captain Zombie said, stressing the point. "That's why when Schoolboy kept teasing her, she may have acted . . . a little . . ."

"Crazy?" I offered.

"Yeah."

"Superpowers can save the world, but only if you can control them," the Ranger said.

"Speaking of which," Keystone grumbled, "head upstairs to the car, you two. We're losing training time."

I smiled and followed Keystone and Phantom Ranger up the stairs. When we reached the door, I noticed that Fiona hadn't joined us. I took a few steps back down and saw her still standing in the same place, staring straight ahead, a worried look on her face.

"Fiona," I called.

She snapped out of it and followed me, though I suspected she wasn't done thinking.

We'll Open the Bidding
at Two Million

In the week that followed, none of the three escapees made a peep. If they'd left town, they hadn't shown up anywhere new; and if they'd stayed in Kanigher Falls; they weren't causing any trouble. At least, not yet.

I wanted to believe the whole thing was over and was looking forward to picking up my comics on Friday and enjoying the Kanigher Kon on Saturday, but I was pretty sure it wouldn't be that simple.

When Teddy, Fiona, and I biked up to Funny Pages, the parking lot outside the store was full. That had a lot to do with the fact that the parking lot outside Funny Pages isn't very big, but it was still unusual. On most days, there was just a handful of cars in the lot.

A large rental truck took up eight parking spaces in one row, and some big piece of what looked like farm machinery filled five spaces in the next row. Jeff had blocked off parking spaces for the news stations, but only Newschannel 9 was there. They were setting up a camera on a tripod in the aisle between the rows of spaces, which made it even more difficult for cars to get into and out of the lot.

I glanced over and saw 20 Questions sitting on the back bumper of the rental truck, reading a comic book while picking his nose. Five other guys—Blubbs and four other comic-book bloggers—talked to one another while they waited to see what Jeff had planned.

As we reached for the door handle, Jeff came bursting out of the store with a portable amplifier in his hand. He put it on the ground, dug his keys out of his pocket, and locked the door. "Sorry, guys," he said. "I need to take care of this thing first." With the amp, he jogged toward the rental truck.

"What is he doing?" Fiona wondered.

"Last week, he's complaining about not being able to pay the bills," Teddy recalled. "Now he's locking out his customers?"

Jeff turned on the amplifier and nearly deafened everyone with a screech of feedback. With nothing else to do, Teddy, Fiona, and I wandered over to see what was going on.

After tapping the microphone and blowing on it a few

times, Jeff spoke. "Thank you all for coming today. I have a very important, history-making announcement to make. My name is Jeff Thornton and I own Funny Pages on Manale Drive." He paused and pointed awkwardly to the storefront for the camera.

The cameraman, who was talking on his cell phone, ignored Jeff.

"As you all know, tomorrow is Kanigher Kon, the biggest, best, and only annual comic-book and science fiction convention in Kanigher Falls."

"What? There's a comic-book convention tomorrow?" a woman in the crowd asked her boyfriend. "Is that why we had to park across the street to get our coffee?"

"At the convention, myself and dozens of other comic-book retailers and collectors will be offering hundreds of thousands of comics for sale, but one will be special."

He paused again, this time for dramatic purposes. At last, he picked up a copy of *Hammer and Sickle Xtreme Team* #4.

My copy. As he turned it toward himself to admire the cover, I could see the small "NB" in the corner of the cardboard backing that kept the comic from being bent or damaged.

"This flawless copy of *Hammer and Sickle Xtreme Team* number four probably doesn't pique anyone's interest. It certainly didn't when it came out back in the nineties. Three hundred fifty thousand copies were printed, but only 2,553 sold. Comic shop owners have paid to warehouse copies of these books for years, knowing they would never sell. So they must have thought I was doing them a favor when I offered to take their copies off their hands."

He gestured toward a stack of four long boxes.

"Now?" 20 Questions asked after an uncomfortable silence.

"Yes, now!" Jeff barked.

I watched as 20 Questions removed the lid from the top box and pulled out a handful of *Hammer and Sickle Xtreme Team* #4s, displaying them for the crowd by spreading them out like a giant hand of gin rummy.

"Thanks to my friends in the comic blogging community, I have learned that 681 copies have been thrown away or destroyed. The remaining copies have all been repurchased by me, along with the dead stock—"

"Jeff!" shouted the manager of Bean There, Done That, the coffee shop next to Funny Pages. "Come on, man! I'm losing customers because of this garbage. If you don't get this stuff out of here in ten minutes, I'm calling the property manager."

"Fire it up," Jeff ordered 20 Questions, who went over

to the farm equipment and flipped a large switch. Things began spinning and whirring, which meant Jeff had to yell even more loudly into the microphone. "In short, I have acquired all 349,319 copies of *Hammer and Sickle Xtreme Team* number four in existence."

20 Questions lifted the first box and hurled it into the machine. After a brief moment of shaking, the whirring deepened. Then a stream of shredded paper flew out a pipe at the top of the machine.

"That's approximately 250 copies down," Jeff announced as torn pages rained down on him like ticker tape in a parade. 20 Questions threw in a second box and a third. "Soon, thanks to this wood chipper, some kerosene, and a box of matches, this will be the only copy of *Hammer and Sickle Xtreme Team* number four in the entire world."

"No way," one of the bloggers said doubtfully. "He only has about a thousand copies there. That's hardly every copy in existence."

Jeff smiled wickedly, as though he'd been waiting for someone to notice that very fact. With a loud clank, he unlatched the back of the rental truck and threw open the doors. Mountains of shredded newsprint with four-color ink spilled into the parking lot like a snowdrift.

The cameraman put down his phone and started to

pay attention, hurrying to get a shot as 20 Questions tossed the last box into the shredder before anyone could protest.

"That will make *this* the rarest comic book in the entire world," Jeff noted, holding up my former copy of *Hammer and Sickle Xtreme Team* #4 so the cameraman and the bloggers could all get good shots. "And it is in mint condition. No yellowing of the pages. No wrinkles or creases on the cover. Nothing but perfection. I will be selling this comic tomorrow. Bidding will begin at . . ."

This time, his dramatic pause really was dramatic.

"Two million dollars. Bids will be accepted at the Funny Pages booth on the convention floor. Booth G-12."

Thousands of tiny scraps of paper swirled around us as Jeff gently placed my former comic into a metal briefcase full of spongy gray material.

The bloggers excitedly typed messages into their cell phones and laptops, each trying to be the first to get out the word that would rock the comic-collecting world.

"I'm hurrying back right now," the cameraman told the person on the other end of his phone. "Call the network. This might actually be something big."

He was right. By six o'clock that evening, the story of the world's rarest comic book was on every newscast coast to coast, from Darwyn City to Fradon. One of the organizers of Kanigher Kon was on the ten o'clock news, saying that they'd sold more than three thousand additional passes in the hours since Jeff's announcement.

"I guess he's figured out a way to pay those bills," Teddy said.

But while everyone else saw a fun story about how high the final price tag would be for the world's rarest comic book, I couldn't help being bothered by the whole thing—and not just because I'd handed over the world's most expensive comic book for six bucks.

As Jeff rang up my weekly purchases, I stared at the briefcase sitting unsecured behind the counter and got a sick feeling in my stomach when I thought about the convention the next day. What was it Schoolboy Krush had said about Shu Fang the panda?

"Why bother with security at a bank when that thing is worth at least a million dollars and it's just sitting out in the open?"

I wondered what would happen with a two-million-dollar comic book sitting out in the open at Kanigher Kon the next day.

99

Conventional Wisdom

As soon as Teddy, Fiona, and I stepped in the door of the Kanigher Falls Collins Inn, we spotted Ms. Matthews. Because it was the weekend, our teacher was dressed more casually than usual, which only meant she'd left the sweater-vest at home. She looked completely out of place in her long skirt, old-fashioned blouse, and tight bun. Oddly enough, this was the one place where she probably could have blended into the crowd more easily if she'd worn her Ultraviolet costume.

Ms. Matthews hadn't been planning to attend the convention, but I'd managed to convince her she should at least check things out. After I made my case, she agreed with me that the world's rarest comic book sounded like a good heist for any one of the three recently escaped supervillains.

"I've been wandering around for ten minutes," she

told us. "But it's so crowded I haven't gotten very far. These tables are like a maze."

It was much more crowded than it had ever been in previous years. In the past, there had always been plenty of room to walk, but now every aisle of tables was jam-packed with people.

"Where's this comic book?" Ultraviolet asked, clearly eager to do whatever needed to be done and leave the convention for more important things.

"Booth G-12," I said as I opened the convention guidebook they'd given us at the door. Unfortunately, the map inside didn't help much.

The hall was about double the size of our school auditorium, but the organizers had managed to cram thousands of people inside. Dealers had each been given an eight-foot-long table to display their stuff, but the tables were organized in a bizarre labyrinth that made the setup at Funny Pages seem well thought out and logical. To make things even more confusing, whoever had drawn the map in the guidebook had added poorly drawn pictures of dragons, elves, and superheroes flying around in capes with swoosh lines that obscured parts of the map.

The narrow walkways between the tables were packed so solidly with con goers that many people weren't even moving. Most booths were surrounded on three sides by eight-foot-high curtains, which made them all blend together in a long maze of drab gray. I couldn't imagine finding anything or anyone familiar in here.

"Ms. Matthews," called someone from the crowd. Mr. Dawson emerged from behind a couple dressed as Joxner aliens from *Galactic Journey*. "I had no idea you were a fan of science fiction."

"I, um . . . always try to take an interest in the outside activities of our students," she replied.

"True, but I hope you're not under-appreciating the value of science fiction as a genre," Mr. Dawson said. "Too often science fiction is written off as 'kids' stuff,' but many of its stories find their roots in classic literature."

"Right . . . ," Ms. Matthews agreed hesitantly.

"I think you'd really appreciate the panel discussion I'll be leading shortly in one of the conference rooms upstairs," Mr. Dawson suggested. "We'll be covering the history of superheroic tales, from Achilles and Hercules up to Man-Ghost and Whirlwolf. Have you ever noticed the similarities between Nightowl and the Scarlet Pimpernel?"

"I can't say I've given it much thought," Ms. Matthews replied.

"Then you'll have to join me," Mr. Dawson insisted,

putting a hand on Ms. Matthews's shoulder and directing her toward the conference rooms. "Kids? Are you coming, too?"

We froze, and my mouth silently grasped for a polite way to get out of going.

"It sounds interesting," Teddy offered. "But I'm doing my own research into the usage of secret identities in *The Count of Monte Cristo*. I'm afraid I wouldn't want your lecture to influence my work."

Fiona, Ms. Matthews, and I turned to stare at Teddy in shock and amazement.

"Ah, yes, Alexandre Dumas," Mr. Dawson said, pronouncing the author's name with a French accent. "Sounds fascinating, Teddy. I look forward to reading it." He tugged at Ms. Matthews's arm and led her away. She cast an envious look back at us.

"Where did you come up with that?" Fiona asked, her voice tinged with disbelief.

"I read it on some comic blog a few months ago," he answered matter-of-factly while examining the map further. He pointed to a spot near a picture of an elf with a bow and arrow. "The Heroguys booth with the con-exclusive action figures is right by the red entrance."

"But we're not sure if this is the red or blue entrance," I reminded him.

"No, I see what you mean, Teddy," Fiona said. "If we go two rows to our left and it's there, we'll know this is the red entrance, and then we'll know how to get to Funny Pages."

"Huh?" Teddy mumbled. "Oh, yeah, I guess that works, too. If we want to get those Red Terra figures, we need to get there early."

We headed down the first row and hung a left, passing through the role-playing game area. People repeatedly offered us free twenty-sided dice in the hopes we might stop to look at the newest games. "If you play Scimitars & Savages, you can be an evil troll priest with impenetrable armor," one offered.

"If you play Marshals & Myrmidons, you can be an armored troll priest that's evil," another countered, handing us each a twenty-sided die. Fiona and I gave our dice to Teddy.

"One more row and we should be able to see the—"

A cloaked figure stood before us, wielding a long-handled ax. Fiona threw out an arm to stop me, but I had already seen the threat and tried to stop so fast I wound up toppling over backward.

"What business have you in these woods?" the axman asked in a familiar voice.

"Woods?" I groaned.

Dave Bargman stared down at me from beneath a dark hooded cloak. He pointed a threatening finger at us while leaning on the handle of a battle-ax that was taller than he was.

"Wizard!" he bellowed into my face. "You shall not pass!"

16

That's How I Roll

"Jeez, Dave, watch what you're doing there," I said, standing up and brushing some of the lint from the cheap carpet off my pants.

"Dave?" Dave said in what had to be about the deepest voice he could manage. "Dave's not here, squire. My name is Lord Überawesome the Cunning, and you be my prisoners."

Fiona pushed the ax aside. "We don't have time for this, Dave."

A bigger kid, who I recognized from the ninth grade, stepped up behind Dave. "Is there a problem here, knave?" he asked with a menacing chuckle.

"Please play along," Dave begged us in a whisper. "I need to capture some prisoners. It'll take five minutes." He gave us a look that would have made a puppy feel sorry for him.

Fiona sighed loudly.

"None, Sir Randy!" Dave told the ninth grader. "I found these three infiltrating the kingdom, but they were quickly subdued."

"Interlopers, eh?" Sir Randy hissed. "Good job, Putrid. I'll take them to the king."

"I thought your name was Überawesome," I said, trying not to laugh.

"While I appreciate the offer, I can take them to the king myself," Dave insisted.

The ninth grader frowned at the suggestion. "Insubordination, Putrid?" He reached into the pocket of his cloak and withdrew a suede pouch. He opened it and held up a black, diamond-shaped ten-sided die. "As commander of the guard, I order you to groom and wash my horse and clean out his stable, losing you"—he rolled the black die and read the white four aloud—"four charisma points."

Dave dropped his head in defeat, took a sheet of paper from his pocket, unfolded it, erased a number, and wrote in his new score.

With smug satisfaction, Randy informed us that we were his prisoners and that we had a meeting with the king.

"I don't think so," I protested.

"Yeah, we're not here to play your stupid game," Teddy said. "We have an exclusive Red Terra figure we need to get before the line's too long."

But Dave just shook his head violently, his eyes begging us to keep playing the game.

"Guys, I know you're not LARPers, but you've *got* to help me," Dave pleaded. He folded up the piece of paper and held it in front of us before stuffing it back into the pocket of his robe. "I'm down to eighteen leadership points. Eighteen! If I don't prove myself today, I'll be demoted to stable boy."

"Fine," Fiona agreed. "Lead us to your . . . well . . . leader."

"What?" Teddy and I asked together.

"Five minutes," she told us. "What are we here for? We're trying to help those who can't help themselves. Isn't that what Captain Zombie or Phantom Ranger would do?"

"No," Teddy disagreed. "We're here to pick up cool stuff we can't get anywhere else, like con-exclusive Red Terra action figures."

I glanced back and forth between my friends, considering Fiona's noble desire to help and Teddy's fierce insistence we move on. Ultimately, my eyes caught Dave's, and I saw the pleading look he gave me.

"Five minutes," I warned Dave.

He nodded eagerly.

We followed Randy to a small area where folding tables were set up for role-playing games. A bearded man in purple robes and a crown examined us from the metal folding chair that served as his throne.

"This is stupid," Teddy complained.

"Silence!" Randy demanded. "Your Majesty, I single-handedly captured these outlanders entering the kingdom after besting them in combat. I now present them to you for sentencing."

"We need to go," Teddy urged. "Can you cut the—"

"Your Royal Highness," I interrupted, adding a bit of a British accent to my voice. I hadn't read a *Med-Evil* comic in years, but I could still remember some of the dialogue . . . kind of. "'Tis aye verily an honor to makest thou acquaintance."

The king widened his eyes. "What business hast thou and thine comrades in the Kingdom of Larponia?"

"We seek only passage, kind sire."

"Yet the captain of my guard informs me he bested you in combat. Why would a simple traveler seek to do battle with my honor guard?"

"Your captain lies!" Fiona yelled. "We were captured not by the captain, but by . . . um . . ." She pointed at

Dave but could only shake her head and move her lips silently, like an actress who'd forgotten her lines.

"Lord Überawesome," I continued.

"Yeah, him," she agreed.

Randy got angry and gestured at me with his sword. "Sire, he doth besmirch my honor. I challenge this rogue to a duel."

"Very well," the king declared, drawing oohs and aahs from other costumed role players around him.

I shrugged, breaking character. "Uh, how do we do that?" I asked, staring at the bigger kid's sword.

A wizard wearing thick-lensed glasses offered me two ten-sided dice and led me to a folding table. Sir Randy stood opposite me, a hungry smile on his lips.

"I roll to initialize combat," he declared, throwing down two dice. A two and a seven came up. "I have succeeded in initializing combat," he went on. "I deliver a deathblow with my sword." He rolled again. This time a six and a five were the result. "Success! You are dead, invader."

"Well, that wasn't so bad after all," Teddy said. "Let's get to the Heroguys booth." He turned around to leave and I started to follow.

"No!" Dave shouted. "He still can make a saving roll."

"Huh?" I grunted. "What's that?"

"If you roll double zeros, you won't die," Dave explained.

"Don't you have a stable you should be cleaning, Putrid?" Randy snarled at Dave. Fiona shot a nasty look at Randy and I could see her jaw tighten.

"Pick up the dice," she whispered to me.

I shrugged and shook the dice in my hand. Fiona stood at the edge of the table between us, waiting to see the results of the roll. I threw the dice, expecting to be dead and hoping that would allow us to leave and get back to finding the exclusive–action figure booth. Instead, I joined everyone else around the table in marveling at the two round zeros that stared up from the dice.

"The outlander has successfully defended himself from the captain's deathblow," the wizard announced. "The outlander may initialize if he wishes."

Again, I shrugged, not knowing what they were talking about.

"You can attack him now," Dave said. "But since you don't have a recognized character within the realm, you'll need to roll a nine or a zero."

I decided I might be better off if I stopped trying to understand Dave's explanation and just rolled the die.

Fiona looked sick, like she was getting ready to throw up, but she gave me a nod. I looked down at her right hand, resting on the edge of the table, and saw the blue ring on her middle finger. Suddenly, I understood what was happening.

I threw the dice and got the nine I needed. What I didn't see—what no one else at the table saw—was Fiona using the ring to slow time for herself, reaching out for the dice between the milliseconds, and positioning them on the necessary numbers.

I needed two nines to strike the captain, and Fiona made sure I got them. The captain could have fended it off by rolling anything higher than a four, but Fiona gave him a three. Then she gave me the nineteen I needed to continue my assault and the twenty it took to drop him to his knees.

"Amazing," the wizard yelled out.

"This can't be happening." Sir Randy raged, throwing his sword to the ground with a tinny clatter.

"Another nineteen or twenty and the captain of the guard is defeated," the wizard informed the crowd.

I shook the dice and gave Fiona a glance. Her face was pale and her eyelids were drooping. The Ring of Mercury was still too much for her to handle for more than a few minutes.

With a vigorous shake, I clenched my fist and raised the dice above my head. "Your Majesty!" I shouted. "I sayeth again that I be no more than a traveler. The death of your captain proves not my innocence, so I stay my weapon." I handed the dice to Dave. "Lord Überawesome, I relinquish my sword to you."

The angry ninth grader threw his dice again. "I roll to initialize combat with the knave Putrid!"

"Defensive strike," Dave shouted as he rolled the dice I'd handed him.

The dice came to rest on the table, eighteen to five in Dave's favor.

A cheer rose from the crowd. Meanwhile, Fiona was struggling to stay on her feet. The ring was back on a chain around her neck instead of on her finger, and she was scarfing down a box of raisins as though her life depended on it. That was when I realized she hadn't been able to tip the scales in Dave's favor.

"No, it's not fair," Randy cried out.

"Good show, Putrid," the king said happily. "Or should I say, Lord Überawesome? As a reward, I grant you any wish within my power to grant."

Dave turned to us. "Good sire, please grant these travelers safe passage through thy kingdom."

"Indeed," the king agreed. "Travelers, you shall always be welcome in the lands of Larponia. When you need us, you can always count on the power of King Hemlock."

"And my ax," Dave added.

Fiona, Teddy, and I smiled and waved as we made our way through the role-playing area.

"Did any of that make any sense to either of you?" Teddy asked nervously as we left.

I shook my head but couldn't help noticing Fiona's confident smile.

"That's a relief," Teddy said to me. "I thought it was only me."

Facts and (Action) Figures

It didn't take as long as I'd thought it would to get to the action figure booth. That meant we also had an idea of where the Funny Pages booth was, so we could head that way as soon as we got our exclusive Red Terras.

For the moment, I was putting all my worries about supervillains and million-dollar-comic heists out of my mind. Dozens of Red Terra figures were stacked up on the table, and only three people were in front of us. Teddy had been smart to make sure we got there early enough to guarantee—

"Hey, kid, what do you think you're doing?" a gruff voice shouted from behind us.

I turned to see a squat man in a Nightowl shirt staring a hole right through us. "We're in line to buy these figures," I explained.

"They're con exclusives," Fiona added.

"Yeah, I know that," the man said. "That's why I'm in line for one. That's why all of us are in line for one." He gestured to a stream of people behind him that stretched into the crowded convention hall. It was impossible to tell where the line ended.

"This is the *front* of the line," he said. "The back of the line is that way."

Sheepishly, we walked toward the end under the constant glare of people who thought we had been trying to cut in line.

"This is pointless," Fiona complained as we reached the last person after what seemed like an endless march.

"Then go do something else," Teddy suggested. "I'm staying here just in case."

"There are probably two hundred people in front of us," she pointed out. "They only have one hundred exclusive figures to sell."

"There aren't that many people," I said, disagreeing.

"And maybe not everyone in line is getting a figure," Teddy said, hoping aloud.

"Why else would they be in line?" Fiona asked.

"They could be keeping their friends company . . . without complaining," Teddy grumbled.

As much as I wanted Teddy to be right, that hope dimmed with every person I saw walk past carrying a big plastic package with the Red Terra logo across the top. He might be right that not all the people in line were fans, but many of them were likely there because they knew that an exclusive fifteen-dollar figure could sell for more than a hundred dollars on eBay.

"Maybe they have more in the back," I said unconvincingly.

"In the back of where?" Fiona argued. "It's an eight-foot-wide booth. There's not exactly room for a warehouse."

She was right again, but I still refused to get out of line.

"Besides," she went on, "the whole point of limited-edition figures is that they are *limited*. If they could just go get more in the back, it wouldn't be special, would it?"

It was less than a half hour into the convention, and I already was facing my first disappointment of the day. I'd had the money for that action figure set aside for two months and never considered that I might not get one.

"You know, we're supposed to be finding Jeff's booth so we can warn him," Fiona reminded us.

"And why do we need to warn him right now? You sure didn't seem too concerned about wasting time when we had to shoot dice with the Knights of the Dork Table," Teddy snapped. "If Ultr—if Ms. Matthews can take an hour or two to go listen to Mr. Dawson's lecture, we can stand in line for twenty minutes to get a limited-edition

Red Terra." He pointed toward the entrance we'd come through. "If Terrorantula is going to walk through the door, we'll definitely see him, and then we'll go warn Jeff."

"What if he comes in the blue entrance?" Fiona said.

Teddy bit his lower lip. "Which one is the blue entrance again?"

Fiona threw up her hands in frustration and turned her back on Teddy.

A woman in a black T-shirt with a white Heroguys logo on the chest walked down the line of people waiting, counting to herself. She would stop to talk briefly with groups of people together and nodded to each person who answered. As she got closer, I could overhear her talking to the people in front of us.

"Ninety-three. Ninety-four. Are you going to all be purchasing Red Terra figures?"

"Only me," a man dressed in a *Galactic Journey* armada uniform answered.

"Then you're ninety-five. Ninety-six. Ninety-seven."

She reached us.

"Are all three of you planning to purchase the limited-edition Red Terra figure?"

"I'm not," Fiona groaned.

"I am," Teddy and I replied together.

"Ninety-eight and ninety-nine, then. And you are

number one hundred," she told the man behind us. He pumped his fist in celebration while the people behind him grimaced in agony and dismay.

"Is there any chance you have more in the back?" one of them pleaded.

"No, I'm afraid not," the woman from the toy company said. "Of course, you're welcome to stay in line in case someone decides not to wait and gives up his spot."

"Fat chance of that," Teddy laughed as most of the line that stretched out behind us dispersed, leaving only a half dozen or so hopefuls.

Whatever disappointment I'd felt earlier had been washed away. We inched forward, nearing the bend in the line that would put us in view of the Heroguys booth and give us our first good look at the figure we'd been waiting so long for.

"Do you see what I see?" Fiona asked.

"Not yet," Teddy eagerly replied. "About two more people and I think I'll be able to make out the side of the package."

"No, not the booth, dummy." She grabbed me by the arm and pointed at the red entrance.

Beneath the big number 2 that hung over the entrance stood three men. One was huge and wore a tight schoolboy's outfit. The second hid his face behind a shielded helmet and wore a red leather jacket with a spider on the left shoulder. The third wore an old, torn T-shirt with the sleeves cut off and a dirty bandana that did nothing to keep his long, stringy hair out of his face. He smiled to show a mouthful of teeth filed to points. All three of the escaped supervillains were at the convention, and they appeared to be working together.

Schoolboy Krush cracked his knuckles and made a move to begin plowing through the overly crowded aisles, but Terrorantula held up a hand to stop him. I couldn't hear what they were saying, but whatever it was made Schoolboy look disappointed.

"Maybe they're fans in costumes," Teddy proposed. "We really don't have any way of telling. I think you should keep an eye on them and I'll stay in line and join you once I have my Red Terra figure."

Screamfang had a different reaction to Terrorantula. He threw back his head and laughed, then ran his tongue across the sharp ridges in his wide-open mouth before taking off on his own.

Since none of them were using their powers yet, the monitor in my pocket hadn't gone off. That meant Ms. Matthews, sitting in Mr. Dawson's lecture, had no idea they were here.

"Excuse me. Pardon. Excuse me, I just want to get

past here," Screamfang said as he neared the line where we were still standing. "Come on, people! Can't we move any faster than this?"

A man in a Man-Ghost T-shirt with holes in the armpits stopped Screamfang to take a photo. "Wow, those teeth look real," the man said, obviously impressed. "You look just like him."

"Uh, thanks?" Screamfang accepted the compliment and pushed his way slowly through the rest of the crowd.

"Come on, we have to go after him," Fiona ordered.

There were only fifteen people left in front of us in line. The Heroguys booth was so close, with smiling staff members holding Red Terra figures in both arms, ready to hand them over.

Fiona saw me staring longingly at the figures, and she smacked me in the chest. "Oh, you are not serious. Come on, he's getting away." She dragged me out of line and coaxed Teddy to follow us.

Teddy looked back and forth between us and the Heroguys booth. "I'll be right behind you," he finally said, holding his ground and turning back to the booth.

With an angry huff, Fiona dragged me away. The 101st guy in line let loose an enthusiastic "Yee-es!" and thrust both arms over his head.

At least if Teddy got the exclusive figure, I could still

look at it. I'd probably get to touch it, too, since Teddy wouldn't be able to keep the collector's item in the box for more than a few days before temptation got the better of him.

We did our best to follow Screamfang, who was headed in the general direction of the back corner where the Funny Pages booth was supposed to be. Tracking him proved more difficult than we'd anticipated, though, considering we couldn't see much farther than three people in front of us.

"He had to have gone this way," Fiona reasoned. "He might have gone down a different aisle, but we know where he's heading." After a few twists and turns, we found row G.

There was no sign of Screamfang, but there was no sign of Jeff or the Funny Pages booth, either. In the entire row, there were no booths selling comics at all.

Instead, model planets and spaceships hung from the ceiling, and each booth was plastered with starscapes.

It wasn't until we were halfway down the row and standing at booth G-12 that we realized where we were. An older bald man sat behind the table at G-12. I wasn't a fan of *Galactic Journey,* but even I recognized Captain Lindstrom, or rather Sven Ryan, the actor who played Captain Lindstrom.

The Final Frontier

"Hello, cadets." The actor welcomed us in the deep, rich tone that was Captain Lindstrom's trademark.

"Uh . . . hi," I said, looking around for some kind of indication of what we'd done wrong. At the top of the booth, though, was a little cardboard sign that read G-12.

"Were you looking to get an autograph?" He swept his hand across stacks of glossy photos of him in his Captain Lindstrom uniforms, as well as one photo of him in tights and a tunic. "From my critically acclaimed performance in *Hamlet* with the Royal Shakespeare Company. Would you care for one of these?"

"No, thanks," I responded.

"No one ever does," he sighed sadly. "It's all Captain Lindstrom all the time."

We kept looking at the booths on either side and across

the aisle, as if looking long enough would magically transform one of the booths into Jeff's.

"Nate?" a voice asked. "Fiona? What are you guys doing over here?"

I turned to see Mark Schweikert. He had decided to wear his red-shirted uniform.

"Hey, Mark," I said. "I thought this was where the Funny Pages booth was supposed to be."

"You're looking for that outrageously expensive comic, aren't you?" Sven asked.

"Yes," I responded.

"You're at booth G-12 in the science fiction section. You want G-12 in the comic-book section. Here, give me your map," he said, holding out one hand to grab my guidebook and picking up a Sharpie with the other.

He made a dot indicating where we were, then circled a cluster of rows on the opposite side of the building that peeked out from behind a pencil drawing of a generic superhero in a cape, standing with his hands on his hips. From what I could tell, Jeff's booth would be behind the superhero's left elbow.

"The *Times* of London said my Polonius was stupendous," Sven said, tapping his fingers on the photo of him in the tights.

"That's mean," I said, sympathizing.

"Stupendous is a good thing," Fiona said as she rolled her eyes.

"It's on the other side of the hall," Sven told us, handing back the book.

"The other side of the hall?" a frustrated voice repeated from behind us.

We turned and saw sharp, gnashing teeth. Screamfang growled at the map as I closed the book and started to back away. Staring into Screamfang's glistening choppers, I made a note to ask Keystone for a crisis monitor instruction manual. So far, it had only ever gone off *after* a supervillain had used his powers. And I still had no idea how to use it to notify Ultraviolet of an emergency.

"Do you know how many times I've said 'excuse me' in the past ten minutes getting over here?" Screamfang moaned. "It may not seem like a big deal to you, but I'm not big in the niceties department." He looked me in the eyes and held out his hand. "Hey, kid, give me that map."

"There are other maps," I protested. "They're free."

"Then you can go get one no problem," Screamfang said. "I'm kind of on a deadline here, kid. There's two other guys trying to find that booth, and I need to get there before they do. So give me the map."

He leaned in and tried to grab the booklet, but his hand was slapped away. He tried again and it was slapped away again.

"What the—" he growled.

I could see Fiona's eyes getting heavy. She pulled me away from him by the collar of my shirt, and as soon as she touched me, everything around us slowed down. Screamfang leaned toward me, baring his teeth, but moved more slowly than a snail, giving me plenty of time to avoid him.

Unfortunately, with the aisles so crowded, we couldn't go anywhere very quickly, even at superspeed. Fiona was fading fast. I had to find a way to help her before she collapsed from exhaustion.

I pushed Fiona's hand from my collar, returning to regular speed. "What?" I shouted at Screamfang. "You think Captain Hart on the old *Galactic Journey* from the sixties was better than Captain Lindstrom?"

The entire aisle fell silent. "Oh, no," Sven Ryan muttered. "Not again."

People began speaking to one another warily. The argument of who was the best *Galactic Journey* captain, Captain Hart or Captain Lindstrom, was a long-standing and bitter one. "Of course Captain Hart is better," a man in the crowd said.

"Better?" Mark laughed to some guy who was wearing a latex nose that was supposed to make him look like one of the Joxner aliens from the show. "Only if you consider irrational hotheadedness the same thing as leadership. Am I right?"

Within seconds, the row became one big shouting match. Some people even grabbed others by the collars and shook them to help make their points about which TV character was better than the other. Four guys mobbed Screamfang, poking him in the chest and bellowing their own opinions in his face.

We started to sneak away, but Screamfang yelled after us. "Get back here with that map!"

"Hurry," I said, prompting Fiona. "They won't be able to hold him forever." We wound our way through the arguing crowd, putting as much distance as possible between us and Screamfang.

"Let go of me!" Screamfang yelled. "I didn't say I liked Captain Linderman or whatever better than anybody! I never even watch this stupid show! I only like *Cosmic Combat*."

Again, the aisle fell silent.

"Oh, no," Sven Ryan muttered, dropping his head to the table. "Not again."

As one, the fans turned on Screamfang. If there was

one thing *Galactic Journey* fans couldn't stand, it was anyone who thought the Cosmic Combat movies were better than their beloved show.

We slipped out the end of the aisle as the shouting resumed, but above it all, I heard Screamfang's threat. "I'm going to get you, kid! What are—Hey, get off of me!"

Not Please—Police

We didn't have time to examine the map. We'd find Funny Pages later. At the moment, we needed to get as far away from Screamfang as we could, but Fiona wasn't up to it. I was practically carrying her past a row of comic publishers' booths.

As we passed Skullboy Comics, Teddy called our names. He held up his Red Terra figure for me to see. "Check it out, man! Thirty-seven points of articulation!" He was so engrossed in the figure, he completely ignored Fiona.

"Can you help me out here?" I snapped, trying to keep her on her feet. "Fiona, you need to wake up," I said, encouraging her.

"Mawake," she slurred. "Legs're so heavy. Canwalk."

As Teddy settled in on the opposite side of her and slung her arm around his neck, one of the Skullboy staff members put out a stack of posters and a plastic bowl of buttons with the *Marauder* logo on them. Teddy picked one up but quickly realized what it meant.

"Oh, no," Teddy gasped, bracing himself as best he could. We pushed our way across the aisle, carrying Fiona and trying to get as far from the booth as possible.

Immediately, people streamed down the aisle, pushing aside others, and descended upon the Skullboy booth like a horde of locusts on a field of crops. It took only seconds for all the posters to disappear. The plastic bowl was lying empty on its side.

I had heard some of the adults call them swag hags. They were people who came to conventions solely to pick up all the free stuff, or swag. They had an uncanny ability to sense when it was put out. Buttons, posters, fliers, advertisements, bookmarks, pens, comics—if it was free, they would take it. Free buttons and posters are always cool, but the swag hags will take twenty buttons and fifteen posters and vanish.

There was one advantage to the swag hags' love of free stuff. The year before, Jeff had figured out that the best way to keep the Funny Pages booth clean was to write *FREE* on the Styrofoam cups and food containers from his lunch and leave them on the corner of his table.

As quickly as they'd come, the swag hags were gone, seeking freebies somewhere else. We dragged Fiona through the anime section. Costumed characters watched us with their huge eyes, waving to us as we passed.

"Let's find somewhere safe to hide her," Teddy suggested, eying the tablecloths that covered each of the booth tables.

"We're not hiding her under a table," I said. "We need to find somewhere safe to let her sit down and see if we can contact Ms. Matthews."

"Wha'bout puhleez?" Fiona groaned.

"Please?" Teddy said, leaning closer to her. "Please what?"

"Not plees." Fiona tried again. "Puh-leese." She raised a hand to point at Detective Hemm, patrolling the aisle.

"Oh, police," Teddy repeated. "Yeah."

"No, wait," I said, trying to stop him, but he let Fiona go and made his way over to the detective.

"Officer Hemm," Teddy called. "What are you doing here?"

"It's Detective Hemm," she said, correcting him. "And I'm helping with security today."

"Oh, good, then you already know." Teddy breathed a sigh of relief.

"Already know what?" she asked suspiciously.

"About Screamfang," Teddy said. "Isn't that why you're here?"

"You mean the fugitive supervillain?" she asked.

By now, I had caught up to Teddy. "He's not the only one," I added. "Schoolboy Krush and Terrorantula are around here somewhere, too, but we don't know where yet. Screamfang's back in the *Galactic Journey* aisle. Or at least he was a minute ago."

"Why would Screamfang be here?" she asked. She seemed upset just saying his name, and visions of her knocking down buildings flashed through my head.

"There's a two-million-dollar comic book here!" Teddy reminded her. "And there's hardly any security. It would be so easy for a supervillain to walk away—"

"Teddy, help me out with Fiona!" I yelled as I struggled to keep from dropping her.

"What's wrong with your friend?" a man behind me asked. He was an older man with gray hair and what looked like a burn scar on his right cheek, and he stepped up and kneeled in front of Fiona.

"She's tired," I told him.

"Are you okay?" he asked, looking into her eyes.

"M'okay," she replied.

The man reached into the bag he had hanging over his shoulder and took out a banana. "Eat this," he ordered her while peeling it. "Potassium will do you some good."

While Fiona took the banana and ate a bite, the man stared at me. I wasn't sure where I had seen him before, but he seemed familiar.

"You're the trivia kid, right?"

"Huh? Oh, uh, yeah." He was referring to the Ultimate Comic Book Trivia Championship of Knowledge, a contest Jeff held every year at Funny Pages. I was the three-time reigning champ.

"I thought I recognized you," he said. "I saw you in that store here in town. Funny Books?"

"Funny Pages." I did vaguely recall him. Earlier in the school year, he'd been in the shop and had talked about Nightowl with me.

"That's right." He turned his attention back to Fiona. "How are you feeling now?"

She lifted both legs comfortably, walking in place. Her eyes widened. "Much better. Thanks."

"No problem," he said with a smile. "You should probably get some carbohydrates, too." He searched through his bag again, pulling out some old comics and a granola bar.

Detective Hemm stepped up and addressed the man. "Mr. Neagle, we should keep moving."

"Mr. Neagle?" Fiona asked as she tore open the granola bar wrapper. "Like . . . *the* Mr. Neagle?"

"*The* Mr. Neagle?" he repeated while standing up. "I'm not sure whether I qualify as *the* Mr. Neagle or *a* Mr. Neagle. You can call me Don."

Hearing the name Don Neagle made me wonder what else he had in that bag. I'd seen only the top comic in his stack and I hadn't paid much attention to it.

"Nice talking to you, guys," he said with a smile. "Since I personally requested Detective Hemm to serve as my security detail, I guess I should listen to her. I only have about twenty more minutes to be a fan; then I have a meeting with someone who wants to learn about investing in comics."

"Booth G-12 should be just up here a ways, sir," Detective Hemm said as she pointed toward the end of the anime aisle.

"If you're looking for booth G-12 so you can buy the *Hammer and Sickle* comic, you want G-12 in the comics section," Teddy said, correcting her, reaching for the map in the guidebook.

"No, I want to get Sven Ryan's autograph." He spotted Teddy's Red Terra action figure and pointed at it eagerly. "Oh, and I have to remember to get one of those, too."

"They sold out," I said disappointedly.

Mr. Neagle leaned in close and said, "You need to know who to ask. I'm pretty sure they have a few more in the back."

"Do you think he knows about Detective Hemm's powers?" Fiona asked as they left.

"I doubt it," I said. "I'd guess it's just Phantom Ranger and a few others. I'm sure she doesn't give that information out to just anybody."

Suddenly, Teddy stopped in his tracks. Since I was reading the map, I nearly ran into him. "Good news and bad news," Teddy announced. "The good news is we got to Jeff's booth before Screamfang."

I didn't even have to ask what the bad news was. I looked up to see Terrorantula and Schoolboy Krush standing between us and the Funny Pages booth. They were back to back with their arms crossed, and a laughing photographer was asking them to say "cheese."

Never Make a Deal
with a Supervillain

"Did you see that Terrorantula costume?" a guy dressed as Nightowl asked another dressed as Mr. Enigma, a villain from *Whirlwolf*.

"It's not that great," Mr. Enigma said with a sneer. "He has the spider logo on the wrong sleeve."

"What are you talking about? It's on the right sleeve. You're just jealous that he has a better costume than you do," Nightowl teased.

We pushed our way through the crowd, squeezing past some American Musketeers, most of the Hurricane Squad, and a guy in a white undershirt with SUPERHERO written on it in black marker.

"Excuse me, ma'am," Teddy apologized to a Sisteroid he bumped.

"What do you mean 'ma'am'?" the Sisteroid growled

in a low voice while stroking his mustache. "What? You think only girls read *Sisteroid*?"

The crowd around the Funny Pages booth wasn't moving. Hundreds of people gathered around, clogging the aisle, just to stare at my old copy of *Hammer and Sickle Xtreme Team* #4. Jeff had it in a glass display case, nice and high, so even the people in the back of the pack could see it.

There was no way to get any closer. In other parts of the convention, we'd been able to squeeze around people or gently nudge our way through narrow passages, but you couldn't have slipped a piece of paper between the people staking out the world's rarest comic book.

"There's no way we're getting any closer," Fiona said after five failed attempts to wiggle her way into the crowd.

Schoolboy Krush and Terrorantula were still playing around twenty feet away. They mugged for cameras and struck silly poses, holding up bunny ears behind each other's heads, disco dancing, and building a two-man human pyramid.

"What are they doing?" I wondered aloud.

"I think they're pretending to be opera singers," Teddy answered.

"That's not what I meant. Why are they posing for photos? The comic is right there. If they're going to steal it, what are they waiting for?"

"Think about it, Nate," Fiona said. "We can't get anywhere near Jeff's booth. Schoolboy Krush is bigger than all three of us put together. How do you expect him to fit in there?"

I started to describe the swimming stroke he'd used to plow through the panda crowd, but decided Fiona was probably right. Tossing dozens of comic-book fans across a room wasn't the best way to avoid drawing attention.

Further confirming Fiona's theory that no one could get anywhere near the comic, Ms. Matthews joined us at the back of the crowd with Mr. Dawson close behind.

"Samson. There's another example," he told Ms. Matthews. "Cutting his hair sapped him of his strength. All good heroes have some kind of weakness, whether it's a glowing green rock or short hair. Oh, I wish I'd gotten a chance to discuss that."

Since none of the supervillains had used their powers yet, our monitors still hadn't been triggered. I realized that Ms. Matthews might not be aware of the two super-villains just over my shoulder. I tried subtly to point them out, but Mr. Dawson saw them first.

"That seems in bad taste," he commented. "To dress like two actual supervillain fugitives just days after they attacked our city? Though I have to admit their costumes are amazingly well done."

"They're not dressed up as supervillains," I said, correcting him while the pair posed for a photo in what could only be described as "I'm a little teapot" stances. "That's really them, but if they're trying to steal the comic, they're doing a lousy job of it."

"Maybe I should go get a security guard," Ms. Matthews suggested. I had a feeling she was trying to get away from Mr. Dawson long enough to change into her Ultraviolet uniform.

"No, no," Mr. Dawson said cautiously. "Let's stay here. I can handle this." He gave me a confident smile that reminded me of when he had pulled me aside to talk about becoming a superhero.

"I think they're waiting for the crowd to thin out," Fiona said. "There's no way a person can get close to that comic right now."

"You'd have to be the size of a bug to work your way in," Teddy said, which made something click in my head.

"Or a spiderbot," I groaned.

We all looked at the glass case enclosing the comic. A single tiny robotic spider was making its way across the top. It balanced on the hinge that held the glass front on the body of the case.

"We need to warn Jeff," Fiona said, panicked.

"Let me," Mr. Dawson demanded in his bravest voice. "I'll have to push through—"

In a blinding flash of light, the spiderbot exploded, blowing open the case. The crowd screamed, though I wasn't sure if it was because the explosion had scared them or because it had left a large scorch mark on the cover of the comic inside the case.

Four slightly larger spiderbots dropped from the ceiling on strands of webbing and gripped the comic at each corner with eight tiny metal talons. As quickly as they had fallen from above, they returned to the ceiling, the comic in their claws.

The aisle around the Funny Pages booth emptied as comic fans ran for their lives. I guess the excitement of seeing the world's rarest comic book wasn't enough to outweigh the terror of exploding cases and tiny robotic spiders.

Teddy, Fiona, and I looked up to see Jeff's multi-million-dollar payday crawl across the ceiling of the convention hall and drop into the hands of what Jeff must have thought was someone dressed in a really accurate Terrorantula outfit.

"Ha, it's mine now!" Terrorantula yelled. Little bits of the cover fluttered to the ground, falling from the claws of the spiderbots.

"You mean it's ours now," Schoolboy Krush said.

"Of course," Terrorantula said. "All that's left is to flee, humiliate Ultraviolet, and collect my reward."

"*Our* reward," Schoolboy said, correcting him.

"Sure, why not? All I did was invent the spiderbots, program the spiderbots, and come up with the entire plan to steal the comic. You . . . um . . . posed for pictures? Yeah, that sounds like a fair split," Terrorantula argued.

"What are you saying?" Schoolboy asked guardedly.

"I'm changing the deal," Terrorantula informed him over the screams of people still fleeing the explosion. He rolled up the comic in his hands and slapped it against his palm while Jeff winced a bit with every hit. "I'm going to take my comic and sell it, and you're going to get squat!"

Four long, hinged metallic legs unfolded from a pack on Terrorantula's back. They lifted him off the ground so he could walk over the crowd and out of the convention hall. The alarm on my crisis monitor finally erupted.

Schoolboy Krush lunged at Terrorantula but was held back by thousands of strands of spiderweb. The spider-bots' master laughed and pulled out a remote control for the bots. He folded the comic in half and shoved it dramatically into his back pocket. Jeff made a noise like a dog someone had stepped on.

"Sorry, Schoolboy, you're wearing the uniform, so I thought I'd give you an education. Lesson one: Never trust anyone!" He pressed a button on the remote, and the spiderbots began crisscrossing Schoolboy, like they were sealing him in a cocoon.

Terrorantula chuckled and started to leave.

Instinctively, Ms. Matthews took a step toward the two supervillains, but was stopped by Mr. Dawson.

"Where do you think you're going with my comic book?" Screamfang, his clothes now torn and dirty, yelled at Terrorantula, who kept walking. "Sorry, can you not hear me?"

"Oh, no!" I shouted. "Plug your ears."

I had just barely managed to get my fingers into my ears when Screamfang unleashed a supersonic blast that staggered Terrorantula but did little to stop him.

"Sorry, Fangface, you're going to have to do more than yell if you want to stop me."

A wide, fangy smile spread across the villain's face. "Maybe not."

Something cracked. Then something above us groaned. We all looked up, even Terrorantula.

Above him was a large crystal chandelier. His eyes got wide.

"No, don't—"

Screamfang let go another shriek, which made the chandelier explode in a hailstorm of glass shards. Terrorantula did his best to cover his face, but the rest of his body was peppered with hundreds of pieces of broken glass. Even though we were far from the chandelier, Mr. Dawson stood over us and spread his jacket to shield us.

Terrorantula's four-armed rig wasn't able to compensate for all the writhing about he did as he was pelted by glass and covered in tiny cuts. Then the chandelier toppled over on him. The swaggering Screamfang strode up to where Terrorantula lay in the broken glass, and casually pulled the folded, torn, wrinkled comic from his fellow villain's pocket.

Terrorantula tried to hold on to it but only succeeded in grabbing the corner of the back cover, which tore off completely. Jeff gasped.

"For what it's worth, Schoolboy," Screamfang said, "I told you it was every man for himself as soon as we walked in the door this morning. You have only yourself to blame if you were stupid enough to trust Terrorantula."

He turned back to laugh at all of us before leaving. "Ladies and gentlemen, it's been a pleasure, but I have to—"

He stopped in midsentence and snarled like an angry dog. He had spotted us.

You Mess with
the Con . . .

A wicked smile twisted across Screamfang's lips. "I told you I was going to get you for what you did," he reminded me. Slowly, he walked toward me. Someone in a ninja outfit was crouching near me on the floor. Screamfang reached down, grabbed a sword from the ninja's back, and pointed the blade at me.

"Remember a few years ago when I tried to fool everyone into thinking I was a superhero?" Screamfang asked with a laugh. In an attempt to rob a Federal Reserve bank, he'd dressed up like one of the three musketeers and made up the persona of Commander Cavalier. "I got to be pretty good with a sword. Let's see how much I remember."

He leapt toward me. Ms. Matthews, still unable to change into Ultraviolet, did what she could by pushing me out of the way, but it wasn't necessary. As he jumped forward, Screamfang was distracted by the low bellow of a war horn, which filled the convention hall.

An ax dropped across the blade of the sword, pinning its tip to the ground.

"Nay!" shouted Dave. "If thou dost wish battle with Nate, thou dost wish battle with Lord Überawesome."

"Armies of Larponia!" cried King Hemlock from near a booth that was selling collectible stuffed animals. "Unleash havoc!"

A dozen LARPers charged into battle, swords in one hand and dice in the other.

Screamfang shifted his anger from me to Dave, raising his sword and slicing toward my classmate. Dave effortlessly parried it with the hilt of his ax. "Ye must do better than that," Dave said, taunting him.

The enraged Screamfang swung the sword with all his strength, shattering the hilt of Dave's ax. Another blow knocked Dave's metal war helmet off his head and to the carpet. Dave stumbled back and tripped over his robe, falling to his knees. A sickening grin brightened Screamfang's face. The villain took a few steps back and toyed with his sword for a moment.

"Teddy," I whispered, "do you still have those dice?"

"Yeah." He pulled out a large handful of free ten- and

twenty-sided dice he'd collected in the role-playing game area.

I took them and tossed them toward Screamfang's feet. As he lunged for Dave with his sword ready to thrust, the other LARPers saw what I had done and rolled their own dice.

Screamfang's foot hit a patch of dice and he slipped, rolling his ankle and falling forward. The side of his head cracked loudly against Dave's helmet, and Screamfang went limp and unconscious.

"Wow," Teddy gasped. "I was wrong. You *can* settle fights in real life by rolling dice."

A cheer went up from the LARPers, and the horns blew again. I helped Dave to his feet and thanked him.

"No, thank *you*," he said with a smile. "I am now a knight of the realm and captain of King Hemlock's personal guard."

I had no idea what that meant, but it sounded good and it seemed to make Dave happy.

"Yes, well, thank you both," Terrorantula hissed, snatching the comic book from Screamfang's pocket and celebrating by squeezing it nice and tight in his hands.

He started for the door and I had to act fast. When I'd been knocked down, I had seen the supplies various booths kept stored under their tables. The one closest to me had a large box full of buttons to promote a movie about some teenage vampires who were really hundreds of years old. I reached under the tablecloth, grabbed the box, and tore it open as I leapt to my feet. Then I hurled the box at Terrorantula and waited.

The buttons landed on his head and cascaded down his shoulders and onto the floor. Some slid into his pockets, but they didn't hurt him. He shrugged and laughed. "Is that the best you can do?"

It started as a low rumble, but in a matter of seconds, it built to a deafening roar.

Swag hags!

They swarmed Terrorantula, grabbing every button they could.

"No! Stop it!" he shouted. "Those are my car keys!"

Schoolboy's cocoon began to disintegrate, and the big man stomped toward Terrorantula.

Facing the angry giant, Terrorantula reached into his pocket . . . and panicked.

"Where's—They took my spiderbot remote?" Terrorantula threw the wrinkled comic onto the floor and ran.

Schoolboy Krush knelt down to pick it up. "Looks like I win."

"Don't be so sure of that," Detective Hemm said with a chuckle. "If you want to get out of here with that comic, you're going to have to go through me."

"Don't try me, Maylin," Schoolboy warned. "I know you think you're tough, but you've never scrapped with me." He clenched both fists tightly to flex his arms and chest, further crumpling up the comic. Jeff let out a shout of agony.

"I don't want to fight you, Krush. I want you to think for a second. What makes you believe that the guy who wants this comic is going to come through with his end of the deal? You don't even know who he—or she—is," Detective Hemm pointed out. "What reason do you have to trust someone who won't even tell you his name?"

"Quit talking. I'm walking out of here with this comic now. Am I going past you or through you?" Schoolboy threatened.

"How quickly did Terrorantula turn on you? You guys were going to share, but then he decided he wanted it all to himself."

"You've got it all wrong," he argued. "Me and Terrorantula had a disagreement. That's all."

"I think you mean 'Terrorantula and I had a disagreement,'" Mr. Dawson shouted.

Schoolboy Krush turned to see who'd corrected him.

He locked his sights on Mr. Dawson and pointed at him with the hand that still held the mangled *Hammer and Sickle Xtreme Team* #4. "*You* didn't have a disagreement with Terrorantula. Are you making fun of me?"

Mr. Dawson took a deep breath and stepped forward. He paused and turned back to Ms. Matthews and the rest of us. "Get to safety. I'll try to keep him distracted."

Ms. Matthews rolled her eyes and mouthed "Finally" before sneaking away to change into Ultraviolet.

"First off, whenever grouping yourself with someone else, *you* go last. 'Terrorantula and me,' not 'me and Terrorantula.'"

"What is he talking about?" Schoolboy muttered.

"Furthermore, *you* are the subject of the sentence, so you use 'I' instead of 'me.' The easiest way to remember is to take out Terrorantula. You wouldn't say, 'Me had a disagreement.' You'd say, 'I had a disagreement.'"

Schoolboy Krush stared, dumbfounded, at Mr. Dawson.

And as long as he was looking at Mr. Dawson, he wasn't paying attention to Detective Hemm. The tiny woman, whose head didn't even come up to Schoolboy's chest, reeled back and threw a roundhouse punch into the giant's stomach.

The sound that reverberated throughout the hall was indescribably loud.

Schoolboy folded over, clutching his stomach, and dropped to his knees.

Now that they were eye to eye, Detective Hemm unleashed a vicious uppercut, snapping back Schoolboy's head and sending his cap sailing into the air. He flopped to the ground, and his fingers slowly opened, like a blooming flower with a crumpled and torn comic at its center.

Detective Hemm pulled out a radio and gave officers outside the clearance to move in.

Jeff slowly made his way to Schoolboy's unconscious body. Each step seemed to be more agonizing than the last. Tears streamed down his cheeks as he dropped to his knees beside Schoolboy's hand and wept for his million-dollar baby.

Without warning, a thin white string shot down from above and stuck to the comic. Before Jeff knew what was happening, *Hammer and Sickle Xtreme Team* #4 shot up toward the ceiling, where a spiderbot was perched. Maniacal laughter echoed through the hall.

Not Worth
a Nickel

"At last it is mine!" Terrorantula squealed. "You didn't really think I was stupid enough not to have a backup control for my spiderbots, did you?"

He danced as the spiderbot crawled into an air-conditioning vent, forcing the comic through behind it, and tearing a few small scraps of paper from the pages in the process.

"Two million dollars," Terrorantula sang.

"You idiot!" Jeff wailed. "A comic book's value is based on its condition. Every wrinkle and every crease of the paper drops the price."

Terrorantula opened the visor on his helmet. "So, what are you saying?"

"He's saying you guys destroyed that comic," I explained. "It's not worth a million dollars in that shape."

"Then how much do you think it's worth?" Terror-antula asked. "Nine hundred thousand? Eight?"

"It's not worth a nickel!" Jeff shrieked.

Terrorantula thought this over for a moment; then the mechanical legs reemerged from his back, a bit beaten up and not as elegant as they'd been at first. He used them to stride over the police who were now flooding the hall. Many drew their guns as he made a break for the door, but Detective Hemm gave the order for them to stand down.

"There are too many civilians!" she shouted. "Holster your weapons!"

"So long, Kanigher Falls," Terrorantula laughed madly. "Perhaps things didn't work out for me this time, but I'll be back."

"Wasn't there more to that challenge than just pulling off a big heist?" a voice behind Terrorantula asked.

Ultraviolet hovered near the exit, ready for Terror-antula's next move.

"Weren't you also supposed to embarrass me?" she asked.

"Oh, please." Terrorantula tried to reason. "Let's not bicker and argue about who's supposed to embarrass who."

"Who's supposed to embarrass *whom*!" Mr. Dawson shouted.

"Let's just let bygones be—*Yee-haah*!" Two of the metal legs rose and drove themselves down toward Ultraviolet's chest. She snatched both and fought to hold them back. "Ah, yes! This should prove that Terrorantula is the—Hey, what are you doing?"

Slowly, Ultraviolet twisted the metal away from her heart and out toward either side.

"No, don't do that!" Terrorantula pleaded. "This stuff is very expensive."

Ultraviolet threw a straight jab into Terrorantula's nose, which made him twitch and snort for about five seconds before he finally toppled over and joined the other two supervillains on the floor.

"Impressive," said a voice behind me. I spun around to see Don Neagle. "That was quite a show you kids put on there," he said, looking at the unconscious supervillains. "I mean, I knew Maylin could do that—that's why I requested her to be my security—but you . . . Well, when I was your age, I don't know if I could have gone toe-to-toe with Screamfang and Terrorantula."

"I didn't exactly go toe-to-toe," I said. "And unfortunately, I'm getting used to this kind of thing."

"The good news is no one got hurt," Mr. Neagle said.

I started to nod but then spotted Jeff picking up a few of the tattered remains of *Hammer and Sickle Xtreme Team* #4. "Well, I don't know about that," I replied.

Don Neagle saw where I was looking and smiled. "Don't worry about him. I think things are going to work out okay for Jeff. Remember when I told you I was meeting with someone who wanted to invest in comics?" He looked up and gave a friendly wave. "Well, here she is."

A woman dressed head to toe in pink and wearing ridiculously tall high heels had just entered the building. Colleen Collins stared at each of the three supervillains in what looked like a combination of disbelief, panic, and pain from stomach cramps.

I suppose I shouldn't have been surprised by her appearance. The heiress was known for showing up anywhere a camera crew was likely to be. Considering that the world's rarest comic book was going to be sold in the ballroom of a Collins hotel, it almost seemed a given that she'd turn up.

"Colleen," Don Neagle called. "Let me introduce you to—"

"Nate Banks," she scowled. We had met a few months

earlier when my friends and I ruined her plans to have a supervillain kidnap her so she could meet Ultraviolet. She clearly hadn't gotten over it.

Don Neagle quickly stepped between us and redirected her toward Jeff's booth. "I think I have a great opportunity for you over here," he said.

They started away, with Colleen glaring angrily at me over her shoulder, but he stopped and turned back.

"I almost forgot," he said, holding up a white plastic bag with the Heroguys logo on it, which he'd been carrying all along. He reached inside and handed me a limited-edition Red Terra action figure. "Consider it a reward for a job well done."

It was even better-looking than it was in the photos on the Heroguys website. Thirty-seven points of articulation versus the twenty-four you'd get on a standard Red Terra figure, and he was painted wearing his gaudy 1970s uniform. It was almost tacky-looking, but somehow that made it even cooler.

"I—I can't," I stammered. "These are limited edition. They only had one hundred—"

Mr. Neagle shushed me. He leaned in close and opened his bag. Inside were three more Red Terras.

"They had more in the back," he whispered.

Kanigher Falls Gazette

TEACHER SAVES COMIC CONVENTION
Uses Power of Supergrammar

Three supervillains who attempted to steal the world's rarest comic book were no match for a Ditko Middle School English teacher. Will Dawson outsmarted the likes of Schoolboy Krush, Terrorantula, and Screamfang, thanks to his extensive knowledge of the rules of the English language.

Missing until the incident was all but resolved, some people couldn't help wondering where Ultraviolet was at. Normally, it seems the superhero would of been there as soon as the problem arose.

Assisting Dawson in the capture and arrest of the three supervillains was Det. Maylin Hemm. It later came to light that Hemm, a decorated officer of the Kanigher Falls Police Department, was formerly known as Ms. Mayhem, a supervillain with a past shrouded in mystery.

Hemm has since been suspended from the force, pending further investigation of her past. Until the investigation is completed, a police department information officer said Hemm is remaining in close proximity to Kanigher Falls.

"This is a dangling participle," Mr. Dawson told the class as he drew a red circle around a phrase in the printout of the article on the overhead projector. "The way this is written implies that 'some people' were missing instead of Ultraviolet. Also, people simply wondered where Ultraviolet was, not where she was *at*. The preposition is superfluous."

He continued to circle errors as we did our best to understand.

"'Would of' is not a proper phrase; it's 'would have.' And, in conclusion, for something to be in the proximity of something else, it has to be close to it. That means 'close proximity' is . . . what?"

"Redundant," we all responded in unison.

"Very good." He looked up at the clock. "We only have a minute or so left, so remember your homework on page seventy-four is due tomorrow, and next Wednesday you have a three-page paper due comparing and contrasting the story of a mythological or classical character with a modern science-fiction character."

The bell rang. We got up to leave, but he wasn't done with us yet. At least, not all of us.

"Nate Banks, I'd like to talk to you for a few minutes," Mr. Dawson announced as the other students filed out of the room.

"Or is it a fews minute?" Teddy offered.

Mr. Dawson raised a confused eyebrow.

"I'll see you in the lunchroom, Teddy," I said, shooing him out the door.

Mr. Dawson patiently waited until everyone else was gone, then busied himself shuffling papers while I stood beside his desk in silence.

"I wanted to follow up on our conversation from a week and a half ago," he said. "Given the events of this weekend, I've been seriously considering my gift and my decision about becoming a . . ." He dropped his voice and mouthed the word "superhero."

"And what did you decide?"

"After much contemplation, I've concluded the power of supergrammar may not be a viable ability to meet the everyday needs of a superhero."

"Really?" I asked, trying my best to sound surprised.

"Furthermore, a middle school teacher is a terrible secret identity for a superhero. I can't skip out of class every time someone robs a convenience store or a cat gets stuck in a tree. Can you imagine how ridiculous that would be?"

"It would be difficult," I agreed.

"Not to mention that with all this media coverage, my secret identity is pretty much blown already," he went on.

"That's a good point, too," I said, hoping he'd finish soon so I could get to lunch.

"Mind you, I would always be available if my particular talents were in demand."

I shrugged.

"If Ultraviolet ever needs my help, she can give me a call," he said.

"I'll pass along the message."

○ ○ ○

I made a quick detour to Ms. Matthews's room and passed by Fiona in the hall. She tagged along while I laughingly shared the news of Mr. Dawson's early retirement.

"I bet Maylin Hemm wishes she could just decide to retire," Fiona said. "It's not fair that Mr. Dawson gets all the credit and she's getting so much blame."

"I know," I agreed. "You can't blame people for freaking out a little bit, though, when they find out a police detective used to be registered as a super-villain, especially when the Superhuman Detention Division had just taken three other supervillains into custody."

"Let's hope Phantom Ranger and the others can help her out somehow," Ms. Matthews said. "I certainly wouldn't mind having a little help around here, considering the other thing we know about those three was that the only reason they were here was because there's someone out there that has a grudge against me—"

"Someone *who* has a grudge," I interrupted. "Sorry, I've been talking to Mr. Dawson too much."

Ms. Matthews paused to look at her crisis monitor. I pulled out my own and saw that there had been an accident downtown. One of the vehicles was transporting a liver to the hospital for a transplant.

"If that liver doesn't get to the hospital in ten minutes, it won't be useable," Ms. Matthews declared.

She and I started for the janitor's closet, and I turned to tell Fiona I'd meet her in the lunchroom, but she was gone.

"Where did Fi—?" I stopped my question in mid-sentence as I read the monitor with confusion. The liver had been safely transported to the hospital, and the incident was given a small green checkmark to indicate that it was no longer a problem.

Ms. Matthews shrugged at the monitor's results and continued her thought from a moment earlier. "It doesn't really matter who's behind it," she said. "Someone hates Ultraviolet. And I could use some other superheroes to watch my back."

"I wouldn't worry too much about other superheroes if I were you," Fiona said from behind me. Even Ms. Matthews seemed startled by her sudden reappearance.

My friend peeled a banana and leaned back in one of the desk chairs with a confident smile. "I think things are going to work out just fine."

For a town in the middle of the desert, Kanigher Falls has been awfully cold lately. Sixth grader Nate Banks knows something odd is going on, especially when it starts to snow, and the snow smells like rotten cabbage! It's clear that the supervillian Coldsnap is on the loose. Nate thinks he knows how to defeat him, but superhero Ultraviolet thinks the case is too dangerous. When Coldsnap goes after an American treasure and Ultraviolet can't go it alone, it's up to Nate and his friends to save the day!

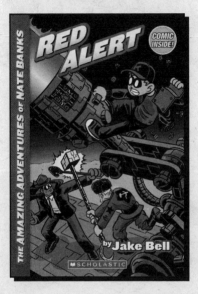

It's winter break, and Nate has finally begun his training to become a superhero sidekick. The only problem is that Nate has to keep his training a secret from his best friends, Teddy and Fiona. While Doctor Nocturne is busy training Nate and helping Ultraviolet set up a top-secret underground lair beneath Nate's school, supervillian Red Malice is gearing up to attack the East Coast with an enormous tractor beam! Will Nate and his friends be able to stop Red Malice before it's too late?

www.EnterHorrorLand.com

GBHL19B

Out of the darkness, heroes will rise...

Also Available:

by Kathryn Huang

by Kathryn Huang & Kathryn Lasky

Read them all!

SCHOLASTIC

www.scholastic.com/gahoole

GAHOOLE15